MISADVERTISED

Benjamin Lloyd

Copyright © 2024 Benjamin Lloyd

All rights reserved.

ISBN:
ISBN-13:

For Linda, the love of my life.
This one was your idea.

Misadvertised

Chapter One

Despite the blaring soundtrack, it had been a quiet night at the Greenwich Real Rock Restaurant, just two tables booked and zero walk-ins. With only four covers and handful of takeaway deliveries to serve, Paolo had sent most of the staff home early.

Now here he was alone at 10pm on a Tuesday night, having to mop the floor of the restaurant himself. He slammed the soggy mop down hard on the floor, watching rivulets of soapy water slosh under the tables and into the shadows beyond. Having to clean the restaurant was bad enough but, but because he was going home early, his wage packet would be down again this month. It was definitely time to find a new job. On the plus side, he would never have to listen to another Adele record at maximum volume ever again. Hopefully.

Lost in his thoughts, Paolo didn't notice the hooded figure emerge from the kitchen behind him. He couldn't hear the tiptoeing footsteps over the sound of Sam Smith earnestly and joylessly warbling out a Donna Summer disco cover on the video screens that surrounded the restaurant. Couldn't react as the figure battered him over the head with a huge battle axe.

Paolo collapsed to the floor, blood spilling from a gash on the back of his head. Stunned, he tried to crawl away, but his hands kept slipping in the claret-coloured puddle that was forming on the floor underneath him. The polished concrete was slick, no way to get a purchase, no chance of scrambling away from whatever, *whoever*, had hit him. Slipping again, he rolled onto his side, looking up at the hooded figure who stood over him.

"Too bad you're not going to be able to *Lick It Up*," muttered the masked figure, pushing Paolo back down onto the floor, pinning him with his foot. Then he swung the weapon again, grunting with the effort before bringing it crashing down onto Paolo's head for a second time.

Misadvertised

Chapter Two

"Listen Eva, the nights are getting colder and I feel like we've been making progress together. Please can I move back into the house? I'll sleep on the sofa until you're comfortable with having me around?" Detective Inspector James Carson bellowed at his hands free.

"No, not yet," his wife sounded like she was crying, voice rising in tone and volume as she spoke, "I don't care if it was for work or not, You *lied* James. You let me think you were *dead*. You were gone for two whole years and not once did you think to send a text or pop me a postcard or something. Just silence. For *two years*. You couldn't trust me enough to tell me what you were doing and that broke my heart James. I don't know if it will ever heal."

"Look love," he tried to calm himself, to soften the tone of his voice, to slow the pace of the conversation and Eva's spiral into despair, "I'm truly sorry. It was an unavoidable, horrible part of the job. I know it will take time, but I'm doing everything I possibly can to win back your trust. That's never going to happen if I freeze to death in the bloody shed though."

"Come on James, you were gone before I even got out of bed this morning. I can hear you're in the car heading off to a case, which means you're going to be out all hours until it is solved. You won't even be at home long enough to talk, let alone sleep."

Carson winced, "Listen, we'll talk about it when I get home."

"No, we won't," she shouted.

The line clicked, Eva was gone.

"Love you too," Carson yelled at the silence, smacking the steering wheel in frustration, "Argh!"

"Well that was bloody uncomfortable," said DS Leyla Hewson after allowing Carson a moment to regather his composure - and refocus on the road.

"Why?"

"Because most people don't discuss personal disappearances and marriage breakdown in front of their colleagues," Hewson tried to explain, "Especially not the ones they have only been partnered with for a few weeks."

"But why not? Is it a woman thing?" Carson asked.

Bloody hell, he's not even joking, Hewson thought to herself, "I can see why you became a cop."

DI Carson shot his sergeant a puzzled look.

"Anyone would think your brain didn't work like the rest of us," Hewson laughed.

"Most of the time I'm grateful for that," the Carson said, matter-of-fact, "And just for the record, I didn't 'disappear'."

"No judgement from me guv," Hewson held her hands palms up towards him. She had seen just about everything in her line of work already and didn't want to get dragged into a domestic situation, not least because her colleagues were constantly grilling her for dirt on their new boss, "None of my business, not my problem. And quite honestly, I don't want to hear about it either. This is between you and your wife."

"One word of warning though Hewson," Carson said, giving her a steely sideways look, "probably best not to mention any of this to our colleagues. Operational secrets and all that."

Hewson made a cartoon gesture of zipping her mouth shut, all the while wondering how a domestic argument classified as an 'operational secret', even if he was her boss. She turned her attention to the traffic, scanning every car as she always did, looking for a specific silver vehicle.

Carson pulled the car to a halt behind a large white police van and jumped out as though the fraught conversation with Eva had never happened, like a switch had been flicked and he'd leapt straight into 'cop' mode. Hewson scurried to catch up as they strode through a scattering of lightweight steel patio tables and chairs towards a chrome-framed glass door.

"Real Rock Restaurants," Hewson read the neon sign aloud, "Your sort of place, sir?"

"Only the first two-thirds," Carson replied, "Something these places no longer have."

"I never took you for a fan of cheesy chain restaurants, guv."

"Once upon a time these places were super cool, Detective Sergeant," Carson said wistfully, "Rock stars really came here to eat. Sometimes they even played impromptu gigs for their fellow diners."

"Back in the last century I'm guessing?"

"Oh yes, the first one opened in the early 1970s, the very epitome of rock star cool. But I doubt any self-respecting artist would be seen dead here these days. I know I wouldn't. Now it's all about branded t-shirts, crap cocktail glasses and staring at loud pop music videos while munching generic burgers and ignoring your dining companions."

Carson' seemed to be preparing to launch into a rant, but was thankfully interrupted by a fluorescent-jacketed PC, apparently one of the first on the scene. The female officer's face was pale and drawn and she smelled like vomit, a few lumps of recycled breakfast caught in the strands of black hair that had escaped from under her bowler hat. She spoke like she was having a waking nightmare, "WPC Jayawardene sir. We got the call from the day shift manager who arrived to unlock and set up for lunch."

The WPC paused to gesture to a woman sat at one of the outdoor tables, tearful and traumatised, "She found the body and called us immediately. We were super careful not to touch anything sir. And we made sure we all threw up out here in the bushes. But…"

Her voice trailed off as she tried hard not to remember what she had seen. Carson was recording everything in his notebook, a long series of bullet points that would continue to grow until the case was solved. The strangest thing was that although they had only worked together for a few weeks, Hewson had rarely seen Carson refer back to his notes. It was like turning events into written words created an indelible record in his memory.

Carson nodded his thanks to WPC Jayawardene, then continued towards the restaurant. They walked past another uniformed officer dutifully vomiting into one of the potted palm trees that dotted the patio and in through the restaurant door. Hewson tried not to smirk at the young copper's discomfort. Carson didn't even seem to notice.

Inside, it looked like an abattoir. Or what Hewson imagined an abattoir run by Freddy Krueger and Michael Myers would look like. Her stomach lurched, she didn't feel like smirking any more. There was blood splattered on every surface, from fine droplets to significant arterial spray, floor to ceiling. Like someone had used a garden sprinkler to redecorate the restaurant. Puddles of congealing red spread across the polished cement, drawing their eyes to the victim who was splayed in the middle of the floor. He was laid on his back, arms outstretched, posed in total surrender. He was also conspicuously missing his head, helping to explain the source of all the blood.

Leaned up against the table nearest the body was a large battle-axe. On closer examination she realised it was actually a 4-string bass guitar, one side shaped and painted to look like a battle-axe. In amongst the copious amounts of blood smeared on the instrument, Hewson could just make out the black sharpie smudge of an autograph. Gene Simmons.

"Well, someone had a *crazy, crazy night*," Carson noted drily.

Chapter Three

For a moment Hewson thought *she* might vomit. She'd been to plenty of murder scenes before, but nothing like this. Back in her uniform days some of her colleagues had been to road traffic accidents, witnessed drivers decapitated when their speeding cars had become trapped under lorries. None of those officers had ever been truly the same again, and now she finally understood why.

Thankfully, Derek Shaw the senior scene of crime officer (SOCO) arrived just then to take her mind off the horrific scarlet tableau before her. He was wearing his usual disposable blue forensic suit, blue eyes twinkling merrily above the mask and a curl of greying hair trying to escape from his hood. Hewson realised she had never actually ever seen the rest of Shaw's face, wouldn't recognise him if he walked past in the street.

"Looking a little green there, Hewson and not a shade that compliments the claret," Shaw noted, gesturing at the spray-patterned walls, "Do you need to step out for a moment before you ruin my crime scene?"

"No. No, I'll be fine," she stuttered, fighting the rising bile. *Deep breath, take a deep breath Hewson.*

Shaw stared at her for a moment longer, then started a preliminary walkthrough of the restaurant floor. He unslung the digital camera from his neck, completing a lap of the body, snapping a steady stream of pictures of the corpse and the bloodied guitar. Every time the camera flashed, another grotesque freeze frame image was burned into Hewson memory. Shaw continued walking backwards, away from the front door, heading towards the kitchen at the rear, following a trail of smeared, bloody footprints.

Click, flash. Click, flash. Click, flash.

"Did you see this Carson?" he asked, pointing at the wall. A brass plaque announced that the smashed glass case had previously contained a bass guitar owned and played by Gene Simmons of Kiss. On the wall below someone had daubed the word "YES!" in blood. The adjacent case had also been smashed, the white dress inside, once worn by Adele, had been daubed with "NO!".

"Curious," agreed Carson.

"Bloody weird," added Hewson.

Shaw made his way back to the body, snapping more pictures as he went. He completed one more lap of the body, then squatted down on his haunches.

"OK Carson," he started, "Obviously this all has to go back to the crime lab for proper analysis along with an official autopsy but here are my initial observations. First, the guitar is the murder weapon - the victim was definitely alive when the perp started hacking with the blade. Looks like he took an incapacitating blow or two to the back of the head before the killer really set to work. Second, the 'blade' is ridiculously dull, it would have taken bloody ages to chop through, so he held the vic down with his foot while he swung the guitar again and again and again."

"Bloody bloody ages indeed," Carson murmured.

"Don't interrupt," Shaw chided him, "I'm not done yet. The third you need to note is that the victim's head is missing."

"Do you think the killer took it with him?" Carson asked.

Hewson could feel her stomach starting to turn again. She tried not to look at the torn and mutilated flesh sticking out of the victim's collar.

"It's possible. And finally," Shaw began like he was about to pull a rabbit out of a hat, "Our perp is clearly forensically aware. Of course I will have my team dust the area, but I'm almost certain he hasn't left us any fingerprints. Worse still, the smudged footprints indicate he was wearing shoe covers. I would be willing to bet he was probably wearing one of these coveralls too."

The SOCO pointed at his own forensic hazmat suit, just in case neither of the detectives could visualise what he was describing.

"Great," Hewson muttered as Carson continued to scribble.

"So he was definitely *Dressed to Kill*" The DI noted drily.

"Obviously. This is proper *Psycho Circus* stuff. Now if you're quite done, get the hell off my scene. Please," demanded Shaw, shooing the detectives away towards the exit.

Chapter Four

Carson and Hewson were met at the door by an excitable bleach-blonde man wearing a leather jacket, carefully torn jeans, scuffed motorcycle boots and flashy sunglasses. The kind of outfit a rockstar may have worn in the mid 1980s. Carson suspected he had just pulled up in a pure white convertible Ferrari Testarossa a la *Miami Vice*. He probably even played *Crockett's Theme* unironically to himself as he drove through the grey and damp streets of London. The man was arguing with PC Jayawardene and trying to elbow his way into the restaurant while she tried to resist his onslaught.

"No sir, you cannot come in," Carson said, using his bulk to push the man back into the street. Realising he was outnumbered, the man smiled sheepishly, raised his hands and stepped backwards.

"I'm Max Jackson, the owner of this restaurant," he said, lifting his mirrored Ray Bans to reveal a well-botoxed late-forties face that glowed suspiciously orange.

"And I am DI Carson," Carson replied, "Thanks for coming, you've saved us the trouble of tracking you down ourselves."

"So I can come in?" The man didn't want to take no for an answer, beginning to move towards the door again.

"You do understand what has happened here, Mr Jackson?" Hewson asked, placing a restraining hand on his shoulder.

"Your officer here says this is a crime scene. My day shift manager says there's been a murder. Am I in the right ballpark?"

Carson pointed to the patio table nearest the door, indicating they should all take a seat outside, "We have reason to believe that one of your employees was murdered here last night, some time after closing. Could you tell me who was on shift last night?"

"I sure can," for some reason Max was attempting an American accent - it was making Carson' ears bleed, "As I was driving over here, I rang around the team who were on last night. The only one who didn't answer was the evening shift manager Paolo. Paolo Nunez."

Scribble scribble scribble.

"How long had Mr Nunez worked for you?"

"Honestly? I have no idea, barely knew the guy. HR does all the hiring and firing at RRR. I don't get involved with that side of the business. I'm more of an ideas guy."

Jackson shrugged and flashed a smile, revealing an immaculate set of white veneers that probably matched his white Ferrari perfectly. Hewson already didn't like the guy, wanted to punch his expensive teeth down his throat.

"Fine. Do you have the next of kin details for Mr Nunez?" Carson asked.

"Not with me, no. You'll have to call HR at head office."

"Fine," Carson' pen was still scribbling notes, "Do you know if Paolo had problems with anyone? Were there any staff rivalries, complaints, troublesome customers we should know about?"

"No, nothing that I know of," Jackson shook his head, bouffant hair swaying, "But again, you would have to check with HR to be sure."

"One final question, where were you last night Mr Jackson?"

"Nowhere near here. I was in Hampstead completing my court mandated therapy with my shrink, Dr Jenkins," he cupped his hand around his mouth and said in a mock whisper, "Part of my punishment for drink driving."

"Well, we'll need to speak to Dr Jenkins' to confirm your alibi. If you could write his number in here…" Carson slid his notepad and pen across the table to Jackson. The restaurateur shot him a displeased look.

Carson stood up to leave as Jackson transcribed a number from the contacts on his phone, "In the meantime, I'm afraid that the restaurant will have to stay closed until the crime scene team have finished processing the scene."

"Wait, you're joking right?" Max's accent had slipped, replaced by a nasal brummie tone, "The restaurant business is hard enough right now without the police shutting us down. How long will they take? What about tonight? Will we be able to open for dinner?"

"One of our officers will let you know when you can reopen, *sir*," Hewson said, picking up Carson' notebook and steering her boss away, back towards his car before either of them decided to give Mr Jackson a piece of their mind.

Chapter Five

"Well Mr Jackson was bloody weird," Hewson said as they drove slowly towards the Balls Pond Road police station, "What with his complete lack of empathy and the stupid fake American accent."

"Obviously I'm not good at reading emotions," Frank said, "But did he seem *excited* to you?"

"Perhaps a little. It could have been stress or nervousness though."

"Mr Jackson did not strike me as a nervous person, quite the opposite in fact. And did he really say he was at his therapist's office in the middle of the night?"

"Yup, apparently Dr Jenkins keeps unconventional hours."

"Sounds very unlikely. Check it out."

Carson reached for the car radio, time for the news headlines. Hewson went silent - she knew better than to interrupt during the bulletin. The newsreader led with a breaking story, the gruesome murder of an employee at the Real Rock Restaurant in Greenwich. Details were sketchy, but they promised more information at the top of the next hour. Apparently the Mayor of London's office had already been in touch with the media to confirm that this was definitely not another case of knife violence.

Misadvertised

"Balls," said Hewson as the headlines finished. She was right - it was always bad when the press got hold of a story before next of kin could be notified of a death. Even worse when they couldn't formally identify the victim yet. She could imagine the police station switchboard lighting up with calls from concerned relatives and friends, worried their loved one was *the* one, "Big hairy balls."

They had arrived back at the station, a large 1970s concrete box built in a miserable sub-variant of brutalism. The large, grey structure managed to convey just the right mix of authoritarianism and unfriendliness to deter the general public from venturing inside unless they were being taken into custody.

Carson, nosed the car down the ramp into the dark, damp underground police station parking lot, "From the news reports it sounds like Mayor Carnt is desperate to play down claims of a knife crime epidemic in the city."

"Certainly easier than taking responsibility," Hewson muttered.

Misadvertised

Chapter Six

As seasoned murder investigators, Carson' team knew the drill. By the time he and Hewson had climbed the stairs to their office on the second floor, the other detectives had already begun assembling a murder wall, outlining what few details they had about the victim and potential suspects. At the top, a photo of Paolo Nunez, smiling, dark tousled fringe falling over his brown eyes. To the left, a hastily assembled collection of poor quality, candid pictures of the other restaurant staff, no doubt culled from their social media profiles. The right of the wall had been left clear for scribbling, brainstorming and all the other stereotypical note taking that takes place during a murder investigation briefing session.

In the corner of the office at the desk closest to the door where the draughts from the stairwell were strongest, DC "Woody" Oaks was on the phone to Real Rock Restaurants HQ trying to track down a list of recent employees and their contact details. Although he wasn't the newest to the squad (that was Carson), Woody was the most junior, hence the crappy jobs and the even crappier seating arrangements. Hewson gave the young blonde man in his misshapen off-the-peg suit a sympathetic look. He had once confided in Hewson that he'd spent his first paycheque after promotion to detective sergeant on that very suit - one

Misadvertised

of two he now owned. She smiled at him wryly, poor bastard would probably be sent out to deliver the death notice to the next of kin once they formally identified the victim.

DC Witz was busy re-trawling Facebook and Instagram, looking for better quality images of Paolo's colleagues. Everyone who worked with Paolo was still a potential suspects at this stage of the investigation.

Carson strode across the office to the murder wall and addressed the team, "The facts as they stand are these. One victim, apparently killed by decapitation. The victim is believed to be Paolo Nunez, the evening shift manager at the Greenwich branch of the Real Rock Restaurant chain. Currently we have zero forensic evidence and we don't really expect to find any. As things stand, Paolo's coworkers are the most likely suspects."

There was silence.

"And for now, that's all we have," Carson was looking flustered, the lack of an obvious lead was irritating him, "So… Witz and Evans, I want you to go and interview everyone who was on shift last night. Find out if there was any trouble, if there is anyone else we need to talk to. Then you can check out the customers. Woody, I want you to run down CCTV from the restaurant and see what you can get from the other businesses in the area. Hewson, you can chase SOCO."

Hewson nudged him, whispering, "Aren't you going to thank them for their efforts to get the investigation underway?"

Misadvertised

"Oh. Oh yes," he mumbled, before turning back to the team, "And thanks for your efforts in getting the investigation underway this morning. Now let's get to it."

Hewson rolled her eyes at him. Sometimes it was like he needed a parent to remind him of basic manners - or to tell him what to say. But already Carson was distracted, his mobile phone chirping in his pocket, "Yes?"

"We found the missing head," Shaw buzzed cheerfully in his ear, "It had been attached to a mannequin modelling Freddie Mercury's cape. I'll send over some pictures shortly. On the plus side, we're now sure the victim is Paolo Nunez."

"Thanks Derek. Let me know when the body arrives at the morgue and I'll arrange for a family member to complete the formal identification."

"Did I overhear that correctly boss, the killer attached the victim's head to a dummy?"

Carson' phone pinged and he stared for a moment at the image onscreen. Then he turned the phone so Hewson could see - and stared in surprise as she turned and bolted for the toilets.

"Woody," he called out, "Change of plan. I want you to go and deliver the death notice to Paolo Nunez's family then accompany them down to the morgue for formal identification of the body. The CCTV will wait until you get back."

Poor bastard.

"Now we've heard from Shaw, I guess you can get started on the CCTV instead, Hewson."

Dammit.

Misadvertised

Chapter Seven

Hewson sat at her desk, and held her face in her hands for a moment, gathering herself for the next task. She took a deep breath, held it for five seconds and then let out a long sigh. The crime scene had been bad enough, but now she was going to have to watch a man being killed on tape. Again and again and again. She shuffled a few sheets of paper, delaying the inevitable. Eventually she could procrastinate no longer, clicking the virtual play button onscreen.

The CCTV footage from the Greenwich restaurant was easily the worst thing Hewson had ever seen on screen. The killer appears at the rear door of the restaurant, already wearing a full hazmat suit. He even glances upwards directly at the camera, safe in the knowledge that his mask and protective goggles completely obscure his face. No point in even attempting facial recognition.

The man spends a few seconds fiddling with the lock on the rear door, then lets himself into the kitchen, dropping his backpack beside the door. The first interior camera captures him moving quickly between the stoves and shelves and onto the restaurant floor. The man is light on his feet and Hewson is certain that he is moving silently.

Switching to the next camera, Paolo appears in the field of view, back turned to the kitchen door. He doesn't notice the swing door opening and closing, the shadowy figure slinking into the restaurant proper. The masked man pauses and swings his elbow at the wall, retrieving the axe-shaped guitar from the broken display case. No reaction from Paolo, the music too loud to hear the breaking glass falling to the floor.

A few silent steps and the man is right behind Paolo. He raises the axe, bringing it down on the top of Paolo's head. The restaurant manager collapses instantly, face down. He makes a few attempts to crawl away, slipping repeatedly in the pool of blood spreading from his head wound. He rolls onto his side as the killer takes another step and uses his foot to push Paolo flat on his back. Then he swings again with the axe. And again. And again. And again.

Finally Paolo's head separates from his body skittering a few feet across the floor and there is a gush of blood, spreading rapidly outwards. The killer's suit is covered in spatter as he bends down to retrieve the head. He moves to the other side of the restaurant and places the severed head proudly on the Freddie Mercury mannequin, standing back for a moment, hands on hips, admiring his handiwork. Then he walks back towards the kitchen, pausing at the display cabinets to daub his bloody message on the walls.

Switching back to the first camera in the kitchen, and Hewson watches as the man retrieves a large sheet of plastic from his red and black rucksack, spreads it out on the floor, then steps into the middle. He peels off the blood-soaked clothing to reveal what looks like motorbike leathers beneath. Mask, goggles and plastic gloves are tossed onto the pile too. A full-face bike helmet comes out of the bag and he puts it on, all the while his back is turned to the camera.

The man kneels down on the floor and slowly rolls the plastic sheet, careful not to spill any blood - or his own DNA. He gathers the corners of the sheet into a double-knot and then secures it with a cable tie. The roll goes into the rucksack, zipped up tight. He puts on his leather motorcycle gloves then he walks out the back door of the restaurant and disappears into the night.

Hewson rewound the recording to the beginning and watched again, trying to spot any clue that might help them identify the killer - or at least point them in the right direction. When she reached the part where the man looked directly at the CCTV camera, she paused playback and took a screenshot. Goggles, mask, hood, full motorcycle leathers. There was nothing to see, not even a brand name stitched onto the suit, but this image would serve as a useful placeholder for the murder wall.

As the printer spat out the picture, she resumed her trawl, inching through the footage second by second, looking for anything she missed last time. A process she would repeat several times over the next few hours.

Misadvertised

Chapter Eight

The day passed in a blur of information gathering, interviews and analysis. The Real Rock Restaurant had been quiet the previous evening with just two chefs, a bartender and three waiters on shift - in addition to Paolo. The manager had even sent two of the waiters and one of the chefs home at 8pm because there was nothing to do.

Witz and Evans had managed to speak to all six employees, none of whom noticed anything unusual or untoward during the evening. And although they clearly were not particularly close friends, there were no obvious grudges that could have led to the brutal scene in the restaurant.

Witz read from his notebook, "One of the waiters named Marv Smithson said, 'It's too bloody loud to talk in there anyway. If you can't chat, you can't be mates - or make enemies'."

"Seemed like a legit observation to me," he added.

"So we checked their alibis," Evans took over, "The two waiters who were sent home early, Allison Jones and Lauren Michaelson, both students working part-time jobs to pay their way through university, and both still live at home with their parents. We checked with the mummies and daddies and confirmed neither waiter left home again that night.

"Meanwhile, the first chef, Danny Chan, went to a nearby casino in an attempt to make up for his lost earnings - the pit boss confirms he lost a grand on the roulette table and left about 1am. The bartender, Ivan Kovalenko, admits he was drinking on the job and went out for a few more at the The Rose of Denmark pub after his shift ended. The landlord called him a cab long after closing and the taxi driver confirms he was taken straight home, some time after 3am."

"One sec," Carson interrupted, "What was the time of death?"

Hewson looked at her own notebook, "Pathologist puts ToD somewhere between 11pm and 12:30am."

"OK, continue," Carson nodded at Evans, pen poised above his pad.

"The remaining waiter, Marv, says that the last diners left around 9:30pm and he and the second chef had finished tidying up by 9:45. They shared an Uber out to Eltham. Yes, they had a digital receipt and yes, the driver remembers them."

"Any chance one of them could have come back to the restaurant?"

"It's possible I suppose," Witz, stroked his chin, "but I don't like either the waiter or the chef for this."

"So, as things stand the staff are pretty much accounted for?"

"Yes boss. Same for the diners. All four had their meals and went straight home, helpfully three of them in taxis. All claim they were tucked up in bed before 11pm. Another dead end," Evans answered, "We've also completed an initial trawl of the employees' social media accounts, but we haven't turned up anything particularly interesting."

"Hmmmmm. What about Jackson? Any suggestion he was in Greenwich last night?" Carson asked the room.

"I called his therapist, Dr Jenkins," Hewson said, "He alibied Jackson, said he was at his surgery in Hampstead for a couple of hours late last night. Apparently he runs an after-hours service for some of his clients."

"Arse," Carson exclaimed, frustrated, "We'll pay Jenkins a visit to double-check, but Jackson isn't looking like a viable suspect right now. Anyone else?"

Evans raised her hand.

"Marv the waiter also claims that Paolo had a sideline dealing skunk. Reckons that most footfall through the restaurant on a week night is for Paolo's pharmaceutical side-dishes, rather than the burgers. So I checked his record and sure enough, he's had a couple of cautions for possession over the years."

"You think maybe he was stepping on someone's toes? Chopping his head off seems a little extreme for most dealers in London though. What does the drugs squad say?"

"I haven't spoken to them yet boss. I was going to do it tomorrow."

"Do that. See if Paolo was known to them - and if RRR has any links to the drugs trade. Maybe they can give us a steer because right now we have zero viable suspects. Maybe they can tell us if one of the gangs likes to mutilate and decapitate. Can one of you follow up with uniform, check if their search of the local bins has found the missing rucksack? It has to be out there somewhere because there's no way a guy this forensically aware took the evidence home with him," He turned to Hewson, "Anything useful on the restaurant CCTV?"

"No, nothing," she shook her head, "With all these forensic countermeasures, the guy seems to know what he is doing. Could he be a professional, hired by someone else to kill Paolo?"

The DI turned back to the wall and scrawled 'murder for hire?' on the board, "Not sure what the motive for that one would be, but right now we need to consider just about anything."

"Was anything stolen?" Evans asked.

"No," Carson shook his head, "Which is good, we can rule out robbery."

"You should probably add organised crime or protection racket to the list though," Witz suggested.

"Fine, Greenwich is run by a Turkish outfit from Efes. You'll need to track down Mehmet Şahin tomorrow and ask him a few questions," Carson nodded, "Three things though. First, be polite. Second, Evans cannot go with you, it's not safe for her. Third, *do not* mention my name."

Evans and Woody traded a glance. *Why?* The young DC mouthed to his colleague. Evans gave a tiny shrug.

"You don't want me to check with organised crime first, Guv?" asked Witz.

"No need," Carson shook his head, "I'm quite sure that Mehmet Şahin is the man you need to speak to if there is an organised crime angle to this case."

"OK…" Witz wrote the name into his notebook.

Carson pointed at the pictures of the bloody 'yes' and 'no' that had been left by the killer, "Any idea what the hell this is all about?"

"Some kind of sick game trying to select a murder weapon?" Asked Woody tentatively.

"Bloody hell Oaks, is that the best you've got?" Carson asked, "There's two immediate problems with that suggestion. First, when choosing a murder weapon, who thinks a *dress* is a suitable candidate? *How* do you even use a dress as a murder weapon? Second, the word is written in the victim's blood. He'd already been attacked with the guitar *before* the message was left."

"Well what's your theory then boss?" Hewson demanded.

"I don't have one. Yet. But you and I will have to go back to the restaurant this evening."

"But boss…"

Misadvertised

Chapter Nine

"And here is the news at six o'clock. Police are appealing for witnesses in the brutal murder of a local restaurant shift manager. Paolo Nunez, 31, was attacked around 11pm last night at the Real Rock Restaurant in North Greenwich." The report switched to a pre-recorded sound clip, *"Paolo was an important member of the Real Rock Restaurant family and together we mourn his loss. When we re-open tonight at 7pm we will hold a short vigil to honour his dedication and commitment to our customers and fans."*

"That was Max Jackson, CEO of Real Rock Restaurants, commenting on the death of Paolo Nunez. And in other news, an Inverness woman has been jailed for three years for handling salmon in suspicious circumstances. Maggie Murdoch, 58, was..."

Misadvertised

Chapter Ten

When they arrived, their path to the restaurant was blocked by twenty or thirty mourners, clutching candles. Young, mostly female and all dressed in black. Some were weeping loudly. An impromptu shrine had been assembled just by the door, surrounded by bouquets of supermarket flowers, scrawled cards of condolence and the ubiquitous teddy bear.

"Are these all friends of Paolo?" Carson asked Hewson.

"Somehow I doubt it," the DS shook her head, "Looks more like an outbreak of social media hysteria."

Max Jackson stood beside the shrine, still wearing his sunglasses even though sun had gone down at least an hour ago. He held his hands aloft and addressed the gathering. Carson thought he looked like a high priest of hair metal delivering a sermon to his black-clad flock, "Friends, we are gathered here this evening to remember our loyal friend and colleague Paolo Nunez.

"Paolo was an excellent person, a true people person who gave his all for his customers. He was a loyal employee, fully committed to helping Real Rock Restaurants thrive. But most importantly, he was a close friend, a man who I could trust. He will be sorely missed."

Spotting Carson and Hewson lingering at the back of the mourners, he quickly added, "And we hope, no *demand*, that his killer is quickly brought to justice."

"'Close friend'?" Hewson muttered, "He told us he barely knew Paolo."

"Hmmmm….." Carson growled.

Sermon over, Reverend Jackson swept through the glass restaurant entrance, followed by the majority of the mourners, some still sobbing pathetically.

"Was Paolo really this popular?" Hewson asked.

"Hmmmm…" Carson growled again, tagging along with the crowd, a mass of humanity surging through the door. Taylor Swift's latest hit assaulted their ears as they walked in, her enormous face pouting at them from dozens of video screens around the room.

Hewson was relieved to see the blood had been cleared up, walls freshly repainted. It would take decades for that particular memory to fade.

"What's that?" Carson asked, pointing to one of the walls. The display case containing the battle-axe guitar was gone. In its place was a new frame showcasing a blue rag of some sort and a crowd of onlookers were snapping selfies in front of it. He elbowed his way closer until he could read the plaque, 'This apron was worn by loyal employee Paolo Nunez when he was tragically slain on this spot, 21st February 2023'.

"Well that's not at all ghoulish," said Hewson, shivering.

"Where's Jackson?" Carson was growling again.

They weaved their way between packed tables of excitable diners, shouting to be heard over the thumping soundtrack. Occasional rock classics interspersed with more modern pop and even a bit of a rap. Lights flashed, video walls flickered, garish colours everywhere he looked. *Like a rock concert without the atmosphere - or rock music.* Frank's jaw clenched. Tight.

Eventually they spotted the CEO, chatting amicably to a group of excitable women who appeared to be hanging on his every word. Jackson was clearly enjoying the female attention, flirting with the ladies, all of them young enough to be his daughter. Gone was the priestly character, replaced by a grinning Lothario.

"...believe the amount of gore there was in here. Poor, poor Paolo didn't deserve that."

"Ahem," Carson bellowed over the music.

"Why detectives, welcome! These are the police in charge of investing the brutal murder of Paolo," Jackson said to his hangers-on, "Do you come bearing news? Have you made an arrest?"

"Not here," Carson barked. His head felt like it was going to explode. "In your office. Now."

"If you ladies will excuse me, duty calls," Jackson said with a wink, "Please grab a table, have something to eat and I'll tell you everything when I get back."

He beckoned to the shift manager, indicating that the flustered young man should find a table for women. Carson grabbed his elbow and steered Max towards the office at the back of the restaurant. Once inside, he pushed the man towards the desk and slammed the door. Carson was relieved to note that the office seemed to be sound-proofed, Beyoncé's latest generic offering reduced to a dull bass line thump that was more felt than heard.

"I sense tension, detective," Jackson drawled in his faux American accent.

"The noise out there, it's a little intense," Hewson tried to explain.

"And the music? Bloody awful. When did you stop playing rock?" Carson elaborated.

"When the cool kids stopped coming in, Detective," Max seemed to suddenly be losing his patience, "So what is it that you want anyway? You may have noticed, we're rather busy this evening."

Carson was scribbling again, ignoring the barb, "We came here tonight because there's a good chance the murderer is here, watching, probably part of your weird vigil out front. But then we happened to notice your new display."

"Paolo's apron? Good, that means the display is in the right place to be seen. So, what of it?"

"Is it really the apron he was wearing when he was murdered?"

"No, of course not, your crime lab still has that. But the apron on display did genuinely belong to Paolo. I bought it from his family this afternoon."

"Bloody hell," Hewson muttered.

Jackson turned to her, "The Real Rock Restaurants brand is built on genuine memorabilia, Detective. *Everything* you see here is authentic - it's what our customers come here to see. So it seemed a fitting tribute to one of our team to be remembered in the same way."

"Bloody hell," she said again.

"Fine," Carson had had enough, "If you see anything unusual or have problems with anyone, anyone at all, you're to call me." He handed Jackson his card.

"I certainly will detectives, good evening."

Carson made a beeline for the exit, elbowing his way through a throng of delivery drivers waiting to make collections. Hewson trailed in his wake.

Chapter Eleven

Witz returned to the table, plonking down three pints of lager.

"Come on Sarge," Woody moaned, "I asked for a gin and tonic."

"The Red Lion is a proper pub Woody," Witz shot back, "the sort of place where one comes to drink actual beer. I know you haven't been a detective for long, but it's time to grow up my boy."

"Whatever," the young man sighed, "So what else have you discovered about our new DI?"

"The desk sergeant over at the Welland Street station reckons he got transferred for inappropriate relationships with his subordinates."

"Really?" Evans was sceptical, "He doesn't have that vibe at all. I get the impression all is not well at home, but he seems devoted to his missus. Anyway, I spoke to Heidi in HR and there's a two year gap in his otherwise stellar work record. He shoots up the ranks to become Detective Inspector in CID with rumours that he'll be promoted to the Fraud Squad. Then 'poof' he disappears for two years. It's like he ceased to exist. Then just as suddenly, he pops up out of nowhere to head our murder squad."

"The DI is a member of a pub quiz team at the Queens Head with Shaw, the SOCO," Witz said unhelpfully, "Perhaps we could ask him?"

"Carson and the Chief Super go back a bit apparently," Woody added, "And when he told us Carson was coming, Chapman suggested there were problems at home. Someone had a breakdown or something?"

"That was my bloody job, and now I find out they gave it to a headcase?" Witz was surprised.

Witz had been acting DI for a few weeks while Chapman interviewed and assessed potential candidates for the role. After a lifetime of loyal service to the Met, Witz had been sure the promotion was his - and he had been devastated when Carson was announced as the new lead detective on the murder squad.

"Come on Charlie, I know it sucks, but no one guaranteed you the job full time," Evans cautioned, "Chapman always said it was temporary. And probably best not call him a 'head case' either. He wouldn't be the first to have mental health issues on the job. How many alcoholics or painkiller addicts do you reckon there are in the Met?"

"I don't care. But I do know head cases don't usually get promoted to lead a murder squad though, do they?" Witz was clearly still seething about being passed over, "Hewson works the closest to Carson, has she said anything?"

"She definitely knows more than she's saying," Evans shook her head, "But she won't betray his confidence."

"Not even to another member of the sisterhood?" Witz laughed bitterly.

"Piss off Charlie."

Misadvertised

Chapter Twelve

As soon as Hewson opened the door to her empty, darkened flat she regretted not accepting Evans' invitation to join the squad at the pub. Obviously they would be doing nothing but trading rumour and innuendo about their new boss, but it would be better than coming home to silence. Crushing, deathly silence that reminded her of just how alone she was.

Hewson had hated coming home ever since her fiancé David died, killed six months ago in a hit and run accident on his way back from the local Chinese takeaway. He may have throughly disapproved of her job, but he was always there with an open ear to listen and a soft shoulder on which to cry when she got home at night. Now she didn't even have a cat for company. Or the comfort of knowing David's killer had been punished for causing his death. She could still smell his presence, faint whiffs of his aftershave or deodorant that clung to the sofa, the curtains, his clothes that still hung in his end of their shared wardrobe.

She dumped her bag and jacket, trailing through to the kitchen. First stop was the otherwise empty fridge to grab a glass of chardonnay which she carried back to the cheap Ikea sofa that they had bought when they first moved in together. Once reclined she fired up the FeedMeNow takeaway app and began scrolling through the options. It was quite late, so many restaurants had stopped delivering for the night. Then the RRR logo appeared on her screen and she almost dropped her phone in shock. The colour drained from her face and her stomach begin to churn like a cement mixer as images from the Greenwich restaurant crowded her memory.

She threw her phone onto the coffee table, and reached instead for the dog-eared manila folder that sat there. She spread the well worn sheets of paper across the table, copies of witness statements, incident reports, crime scene photos, forensic pathology report. She knew every word by heart, but she still pored over the documents each night, looking for the clue that would finally lead her to David's killer.

As distressing as the image was, she studied every inch of the crime scene photos of David's mangled body. After a while, her study shifted from identifying killers to finding some evidence that her fiancé had died quickly, preferably painlessly. The tears welled in her eyes and she flicked to the last page of the forensics report. From the paint and glass traces left behind at the scene, she knew they were looking for a silver VW ID.4. For the hundredth time she wondered if David simply hadn't heard the stupid electric car as he crossed the road. But until she found the vehicle, and spoke to the driver, she would never know for sure.

She dropped the report back on the pile, took a large mouthful of wine and rested her head on the cushioned back of the sofa, feeling the warm tears slide down her cheeks and neck. She was still sat in that position when sleep came and took her an hour later.

Misadvertised

Chapter Thirteen

The lights were off when Carson pulled up outside the house he shared with his wife. All those hours earlier, Eva had been right, he was too late to talk. He sighed and allowed himself through the squeaky iron gate at the side of their semi-detached, two-bedroom home. A quick glance in each of the windows as he walked down the narrow passageway between his building and the neighbour's revealed no sign of Eva. There was no light showing around the curtains on the upper floor either - she must be in bed. As he rounded the corner of the house, he stood for a moment staring mournfully through the large glass patio door. He placed a hand on the door, then thought better of it. Going inside now would only start an argument. It was late, he was tired and he really didn't want to trigger Eva. Instead, he turned and headed across the tiny square of lawn to the small wooden shed at the other end of the garden.

Once inside he flipped the switch on the wall, a single fluorescent tube flickered weakly to life, bathing the space in a synthetic blue-white light. Clothes off, sleeping bag wrapped around his shoulders, he sat on the edge of the small camp bed where he had slept for the past three months since coming back to reality. Despite the miserable surroundings, he was quietly pleased to see that Eva had cooked a meal and left him a plate on the small workbench in amongst his tools. Just spaghetti and meatballs, probably from a jar, but it showed she was still thinking of him, caring for him even. At least, that's what he hoped it meant.

He wolfed down the food, turned off the light and wriggled himself and his sleeping bag into a prone position. Eva was right about one thing, he would be working all hours until this case was solved. It was only the first day of the investigation and already he had a crushing headache. If only he could sleep.

Misadvertised

Chapter Fourteen

Hewson was looking down on a room filled with shadowy tables and chairs. There was something nagglingly familiar about scene and it took her a moment to realise she was watching the last moments of Paolo Nunez's life as he mopped the floor at the restaurant in Greenwich.

But there was no pane of glass between her and Paolo this time, none of the emotional distance afforded by a silent TV screen. This time she was floating right above his head, the smell of recent cooking, sticky sweet cocktails, even a vague hint of Paolo's aftershave hung in the air.

She watched in horror as, right on cue, the masked killer appeared from the kitchen, moving slowly, stealthily, silently. Step after step after step, creeping ever closer.

Hewson screamed with all her might, *He's behind you!* She tried to warn Paolo of the impending danger but her voice was weak, drowned out by the excessively loud soundtrack and the thumping of her own heart. Like a pantomime, but without the comedy, just a stomach-churning sense of dread.

She watched as the masked man crept up behind Paolo, hefting the battle-axe in both hands. The sheer savagery of the blow that landed on his head. The sound of

Paolo's skull cracking under the blow. The iron-metallic scent of the blood that erupted from the wound.

Paolo cried out in pain as he hit the floor and rolled sideways, a look of shock and pure terror as he spots the killer standing above him. He struggles to get away, slipping in the growing puddle of his own blood, all the while whimpering in pain. Hewson is still screaming at Paolo, *Get up, run, he's going to kill you*, but the man cannot hear her. The killer turns his masked face to look at her floating above the restaurant, *How does he know I'm here? How can he see me?* She swears that behind his mask, the killer is grinning as he swings the guitar at Paolo's neck.

Hewson is crying and shouting, her tears mingling with the blood that is spattering on the floor, the walls, the ceiling - and her floating form. She's pleading with the killer to stop, but he continues to hack and chop until Paolo's head is completely separated from his body, a thick lake of blood spreading ever further across the floor.

Decapitation complete, Hewson is spent, completely drained of energy. But the killer is not done. Once more he turns to look at her, pulling his mask down to reveal his identity. Except it is her own face staring up at her. Her mirror image mouth is twisted in a grin of twisted enjoyment.

Hewson screams and screams and screams until she wakes up in a heap on her sofa back in her lonely Kilburn flat.

Misadvertised

Chapter Fifteen

Wearing his trademark top hat and black suit, true crime vlogger Sherlock Holmes was delivering a monologue to camera.

"Tonight on *Homes on Homicide* I bring you news of a new and horrific murder here in London Town. A young man has been brutally - and I mean, *brutally* - murdered in the Real Rock Restaurant in Greenwich.

"So let's start with the known facts. The victim has been confirmed as Paolo Nunez, who was the shift manager covering last night's evening sitting. After an extremely quiet evening, Paolo sent his colleagues home and closed the restaurant early.

"Some time shortly after 10pm, Paolo was attacked by person or persons unknown. From the eyewitnesses I have spoken to, this case is truly stomach-churning, definitely one for the gore hounds out there. Obviously I can't divulge the full details for legal reasons, but let's just say that poor Paolo was *butchered*."

A super-imposed animation of a severed head rolled across the screen, leaving a trail of blood behind it.

"Now let's talk suspects and motives. I'm hearing that the Met is stumped, having already eliminated their entire suspect pool! So is the newly reformed murder squad operating our of Balls Pond Road police station super efficient? Or has the brass made a serious mistake by passing over our old friend DS Charlie Witz for promotion?"

A candid picture of Witz grinning foolishly flashed up on screen for a few seconds.

"As yet, we still have no idea who the new murder squad DI actually is. But if he or she doesn't solve the case quickly, we may all be collecting their autograph on parking tickets sometime soon…"

The picture cut back to a close-up of Homes, "If you haven't done so already, please hit the Like and Subscribe buttons below. And if you have any hot tips or leads, you know where to find me. I'll be back with an update tomorrow, but until then, sleep safe my friends."

Misadvertised

Chapter Sixteen

Despite the horrific news coming from the North Greenwich restaurant, Kirsten Grabowski wasn't concerned. As a proud New Yorker, she had seen her fair share of violence and death - or so she liked to tell people. Most people imagined the authentic grime and crime of *The French Connection* and *The Panic in Needle Park* when she talked about 'home'. She didn't have the heart to tell them modern NYC was bright, glitzy, relatively low crime and entirely superficial. Nevertheless, she was quite sure she knew how to take care of herself if needed thanks to her weekly boxercise classes at the gym.

The evening shift had been quiet, just a handful of well-behaved tables, nothing at all to be worried about. Except that the decline in diners had a direct effect on takings - and they were a long way down on last year. Well below current running costs and nowhere near enough to pay the rent on this glitzy property, just off Camden High Street.

She turned the last of the lights off, stepped out onto the street and began the process of locking up. She had just bent down to insert the key into the door when someone grabbed her purple and green ponytail, yanking her head backwards. A powerful arm looped around her neck, trapping her in a headlock, the man's other rubber-encased

Misadvertised

hand clamped down across her mouth and nose before she could cry out. He shoved her, hard, through the swing door and back into the restaurant.

Kirsten kicked and struggled, but the man was too strong. Occasionally her flailing feet connected with one of the tables or chairs, sending them scraping loudly across the polished wooden floor. The man continued undeterred, drawing her further into the room. Moving quite slowly, he seemed to be searching for something in the darkness.

Eventually he stopped, and Kirsten felt the man release his grip on her mouth. She took a deep breath ready to scream, but he punched her on the nose, the sharp pain shocking her back into silence. She felt the warm trickle of blood sliding down her face at the same time as the icy cold fingers of fear gripped the base of her spine. She suddenly knew with every fibre of her being that she was about to die. Kirsten opened her mouth to cry out, and her attacker shoved something fabric into her mouth, muffling her sobbing pleas. A moment later and the arm around her neck was replaced by something smooth and shiny. Smooth, shiny and getting tighter, crushing her throat.

The last thing she heard before everything went black was the man muttering. "He even called himself the goddam King of Pop, you morons."

Misadvertised

Chapter Seventeen

Carson, clearly wired, was yelling at his handsfree again when Hewson clambered into his car as it idled outside the front door to her flat. It hadn't been a particularly late night, she hadn't even joined the rest of the team in the pub, but the last thing she needed was to start her day listening to another Carson family domestic. She hadn't slept well at all, images of blood splattered walls and headless bodies had haunted her dreams. Especially the one that had woken her screaming. The wine didn't seem to have done much for her quality of sleep either. This case was screwed up - and it was screwing her up too.

As soon as Hewson slammed her door, Carson' unremarkable black Audi saloon accelerated away, merging with the traffic heading towards the centre of London. He gave her the briefest glance of acknowledgment before returning his attention to his conversation.

"Look Eva, I appreciate the food, I really do. The breakfast you left out was great and I love the lunches you pack for me. But I also need to be able to use the bathroom first thing in the morning," Carson was pleading, "Now I'm going to be late for work."

"And?" She sounded like a belligerent child, almost enjoying her tantrum, "I don't care."

"Dammit Eva, I'm back for good this time. I'm back in a regular division so no more extended time away from home. No more secrets and lies. From now on it's just you and me catching up on life together."

"You, me and *the job*," she fired back, "Anyway, I told you. I don't care."

Click. Bzzzzzzzzzz.

Carson growled in frustration, his face red and puffy, his hands shaking with nervous energy. Eva saying she didn't care was like a knife to his gut, probably the most painful three words he had ever heard. Distressingly, he had heard 'I don't care' several times in the past few weeks.

Hewson stared out the window, trying to make herself invisible. She was relieved when the news bulletins came on the car stereo.

"And here are the headlines at eight o'clock. The body of a young woman has been discovered in Camden in the early hours of this morning. Police say that they are treating the death as suspicious and are appealing for witnesses who were in the Inverness Street area near the Real Rock Restaurant last night. Official sources say that the victim has not yet been identified."

The relief didn't last long. "Damn," muttered Hewson, "I guess we're headed to Inverness Street?"

"Carson said nothing, just nodded, driving north as quickly as the heavy London traffic would allow.

Realising that Carson was not in a talkative mood, Hewson shifted her attention to the traffic, scanning every vehicle on the off chance of spotting a silver VW ID.4.

Chapter Eighteen

Carson nosed his car through the police barriers that had been erected at the end of Inverness Street opposite Camden Town tube station. It had taken a while to navigate between the many vehicles blocking the street - apparently the press were out in force this time. Everyone loves a potential serial killer, especially news editors.

"If it bleeds, it leads," Hewson muttered, disgusted by the ghoulish excitement of the crowd of onlookers.

"You know stereotypes arise because they contain more than a small modicum of truth?" Carson asked.

"Oh hell yes," she nodded, "Even if it's borderline illegal to say so."

Carson pulled to a stop just short of the inner tape and was out of the car and under the barrier before Hewson even had a chance to realise where they were. She noticed that Carson kept his head down as he passed the waiting camera crews, like he didn't want to be seen. Actually, she wasn't sure she wanted to be associated with this case right now either. Press fascination would quickly change to castigation if they didn't arrest a suspect quickly though.

"What is it with these restaurants?" She asked, glancing up at the hot pink neon RRR sign above the door, "Seriously?"

"Deadly," nodded Carson, "Ready?"

Misadvertised

The DC took a deep breath and followed her boss in through the door. She paused and scanned the large room beyond, feeling guilty and relieved to see that the room was bloodless.

This time Shaw had beaten them to the scene and was already crouched over the body of a young woman. From a distance she looked as though she could have been asleep, her purple and green hair splayed out on a scarlet pillow under her head. But as Hewson got closer she realised the true horror of the scene. A bright red leather jacket had been wrapped around the victim's neck, strangling her. The woman's lifeless eyes bulged out of her blue face, thick, swollen tongue hanging from her gaping mouth.

"Meet Kirsten Grabowski. This poor lady was unfortunate enough to draw the night shift yesterday."

"Please tell me that's not her knickers in her mouth," Hewson asked Shaw.

"No. He might be brutal and sadistic, revelling in overkill, but this guy doesn't seem to be interested in the sex stuff," the SOCO also seemed relived, "At least not how we know it anyway. It looks like he's shoved a glove of some kind into her mouth. Probably a makeshift gag to keep her quiet."

Next to the body, a message had been scrawled onto the polished concrete floor using one of the crayons that restaurants give to ungrateful kids, hoping it will keep them entertained. A bright green speech bubble, had been drawn to look as though it was coming from Kirsten's mouth as she lay on the ground. The letters were precise, block capitals *WHY DID YOU IGNORE ME?*

Misadvertised

Carson glanced at the broken display cabinet on the wall behind the body, "This guy is a real *smooth criminal*."

Misadvertised

Chapter Nineteen

Chaim "Charlie" Witz's waistline was advancing as quickly as his hairline retreated from a face that had been lived in, hard. The buttons of his light blue shirt strained to contain his belly and his tatty suit jacket no longer did up at all. He may have been just a few years short of his pension, but the man still loved his job even if the salary barely covered his alimony payments to two ex-wives. Their combined divorce settlements meant he would probably be working until the day he died. And in all honesty, that's probably what he would choose for himself anyway. "Death in service" always sounded more impressive than "drank himself to death through boredom after retirement". He'd seen plenty of older officers end up that way, as if losing their jobs meant losing their identities. Considering how much career coppers each sacrificed for their jobs, they probably *had* given up their identities too.

Witz pulled to a stop on the Woolwich Road, opposite a generic looking Turkish barbers, 'Kuşadasi Kutz' according to the peeling sign painted above the shopfront. The sign was so old it still bore a phone number starting 0181. A couple of young men dressed in flashy sportswear and expensive-looking trainers loitered by the door, smoking. A glance through the large plate glass window that formed the front of the shop and Witz could see it was completely empty, not a single customer being barbered. Maybe because no one could get through on the phone to make a booking for the past twenty years.

Satisfied he was in the right place, Witz hopped out of the car and half-jogged, half-lumbered across the road. The young men watched him suspiciously, standing shoulder to shoulder to block the doorway as he approached.

"We're closed," the taller of the men said.

"Really?," Witz looked disappointed, "The sign in the window says you are open."

"Mistake," the shorter Turk shook his head, "Shop closed."

"Just as well I have a key then," Witz grinned, flashing his badge in their faces.

"Why do you want, pig?" The taller man hawked and spat on the pavement.

"No trouble, I just want a word with Mehmet Sahin."

"Mehmet is not here. Now piss off," the taller man took a step towards Witz.

"I'm too old to get into a pissing contest, so let's both pretend you've proven your alpha male dominance and get out of my way."

The taller man stared at Witz. Hard. Eventually he nodded to his shorter pal who went inside and disappeared through a door at the rear of the shop behind the empty barbers chairs. The taller man continued to glare angrily at Witz while they waited. Witz was more amused than discomforted though, for a heavy this guy lacked presence or menace.

Finally, the shorter man reappeared, knocked on the window and beckoned the DS to follow him. Witz stepped inside and swept his eyes across the shop. The barbers chairs and wash basins were covered in a thin film of dust, the mirrors cloudy and dull. It had been months or years since anyone had received a haircut in this shop - probably because Kuşadasi Kutz was a poorly disguised money laundering front. These guys weren't even trying.

Shorty pushed the rear door open, allowing a cloud of foul-smelling blue cigarette smoke to escape, "In here."

Witz pushed past the sentry, into what appeared to be a dimly lit office-cum-kitchen. Three men sat around a table, loaded with plates of meat and salad, grilled vegetables, rice and flatbreads. The DS was sure it smelled wonderful, but the heavy cigarette smoke overpowered everything. Like the sentries outside, all three men were wearing immaculate designer tracksuits and carefully shaped facial hair. The resemblance was undeniable and for a moment Witz thought he had interrupted a family meal rather than a meeting between organised crime boss and his underlings.

When he saw the policeman, the eldest man stood and gestured to an empty seat at the table, a heavy gold chain with scorpion pendant flashing around his neck. He waited until Witz was seated then pushed a plate loaded with food towards the policeman.

"Tradition dictates that we show our visitors hospitality, even the police. So you are welcome to sit and dine with us," Sahin said in a rasping, gravelly voice, watching carefully to see if Witz would respect his hospitality, "What do you want officer? Why have you come here to interrupt my business?"

Misadvertised

Realising he was being tested, Witz picked up a piece of flat bread, dipped it into one of the various dips daubed onto his plate and took a bite. It *was* delicious. "Thanks for seeing me Mr Sahin, I am sorry to intrude but I have come to ask about an, uh, delicate matter."

The Turk nodded benevolently, waving his cigarette to indicate Witz should continue. Sahin clearly modelled his gestures and mannerisms on those of Marlon Brando in *The Godfather* - but his immaculate white tracksuit and t-shirt spoiled the overall effect.

"You have heard about the murder in Greenwich on Tuesday night?"

"Yes, and the murder in Camden last night. Shocking news indeed. One may wonder what is happening to our great city. And what the police are doing to prevent such crimes," Sahin rasped. His entourage snorted in amusement. "Perhaps you are asking for my help to prevent such disrespect?"

Witz shook his head, confused, *Camden?* "No, no Mr Sahin. I came to ask if you had any dealings with the Real Rock Restaurant in Greenwich?"

"Dealings?" Sahin raised an eyebrow questioningly, waiting to see if Witz would openly disrespect him with accusations of criminality.

"I believe you offer 'security' to many of the businesses in this area," Carson had warned him to be polite, so Witz didn't want to come right out and accuse the man of running a protection racket.

"I am a concerned local citizen and businessman. I feel a responsibility for my community, so of course I look out for other firms. They are rightly worried that the police may not be able to offer the protection they need…" the man grinned like a shark, all glimmering sharp teeth, ready to tear chunks of flesh from unsuspecting victims.

"I understand," Witz nodded, trying to ignore the barb, "And do you have any interests in the Real Rock Restaurant?"

"No officer, I do not. Large franchise businesses do not typically need security from concerned citizens like myself. They have their own arrangements that are not so 'community focused'."

Witz nodded. The RRR franchising machine would not be as easy to frighten into submission as smaller, standalone businesses. He imagined Max Jackson would kick up a fuss with the authorities if someone came and smashed his windows and demanded cash. That kind of attention would be most unwelcome for a 'businessman' like Mr Sahin.

"One other thing to note Detective…?" Sahin's eyebrow was asking questions again.

"Witz."

"One other thing to note, Detective Witz," Sahin continued, his moustache bristling with vague amusement, "From my understanding of the security business, which I must stress I am not in, it is always best not to kill the people from whom one hopes to take payment. In fact, an incident like this would look very bad for a person offering security. Other customers would start to question what they are paying for, whether they should perhaps end their arrangements."

Witz nodded. Sahin's argument made sense. No one kills their cash cow.

Misadvertised

"I assure you, I am just as eager to catch the culprit as you are. A maniac like this is bad for everyone. But now if you will excuse me Detective Witz, my colleagues and I have some customers waiting for haircuts."

"Indeed. Thank you for your time and hospitality Mr Sahin," Witz stood and excused himself, grabbing a skewer of grilled meat to enjoy on the drive back to the office. He left the smoke-filled room and walked out through the shop, where no customers were waiting for haircuts. The two men guarding the door stared at Witz aggressively as he crossed the road so he couldn't resist giving them a toot and a wave as he pulled away and drove back towards Balls Pond Road.

Chapter Twenty

"I spoke to Sahin," Witz yelled at his speakerphone as he drove back to the station, "I don't think he did it."

"I agree," Carson yelled back, "It's not his MO. He's not above bloody murder, but he tends to reserve his homicidal rage for his competitors, anyone trying to muscle in on his territory. He also likes knives."

"You know this guy?"

"Yes," Carson did not expand.

Noted, Witz filed that tidbit away to discuss with Evans and Woody at their next gossip session at The Red Lion, "The barbershop is clearly a money laundering front. Do you want me to flag it up to the fraud squad?"

"No need, Witz," he could imagine Carson shaking his head, "They are already well aware of Mr Sahin and the Kuşadasi Kutz barbershop. And his mobile phone repair store. And his kebab takeaways. They have their suspicions about the local taxi firm too. Mainly the fact that there is only one..."

"And Fraud just let him get away with it? What about Serious Organised Crime, are they not interested?"

"Eventually Witz, they will shut him down when the time is right."

Misadvertised

"One other thing Guv," the DS added, "Sahin mentioned a murder in Camden. Nothing to do with us, right?"

"As usual, Sahin's information is good, there *was* a murder at the Real Rock Restaurant in Camden last night and sadly it *is* one of ours. Hewson and I are on our way over there now. Get yourself back to BPR and give Woody a hand assessing the info coming through the tip line."

Carson cut the call and Witz took his foot off the accelerator. Working the tip line, fielding calls from cranks and pranksters was possibly *the* worst job in the murder squad, so he was in no hurry at all to get back to Balls Pond Road. He would pull over in a lay-by somewhere to enjoy his grilled meat skewer first. Slowly.

Sorry Woody.

Misadvertised

Chapter Twenty-One

After the horrors of yesterday, PC Jayawardene had eagerly volunteered for a place on the tip line. She desperately wanted to catch the killer but without encountering another traumatic scene like the bloodbath in Greenwich. Although she wasn't out on the street, collecting intel from the general public may still help to crack the case.

The phone rang and she eagerly snatched up the handset, "Good afternoon, Metropolitan Police Incident Room. This is is PC Jayawardene speaking. Just to let you know that although this call is being recorded, you do not have to give your name or any other identifying information. Now, I understand you are calling with information about the murder of Paolo Nunez in Greenwich?"

"Yes."

It was an older woman, her voice thin and reedy. But there was a force behind her words, clearly developed by years of calling hotlines and helplines, complaining about anything and everything. One of those people you hope you never meet - or live next door to.

"OK... Please go ahead," the police officer prompted.

Misadvertised

"Well, I was passing the Real Rock Restaurant on Tuesday night, quietly minding my own business. And then I saw them."

"Can I ask who you saw madam?"

"Them. The starlings."

"The starlings?"

"Yes, the starlings."

"I'm sorry, I don't understand. Is that someone's name?"

"Well I assume so. That detective bird out of Silence of the Lambs, her name was Starling."

"So you were walking past the Real Rock Restaurant when you saw someone named Starling. What happened next?"

"No, I saw the starlingsssss, plural. You know, the birds. Big flock of the destructive little bastards, zooming about the street outside. Murmurmurmuring of whatever they call it."

"I'm sorry, I really don't follow. You saw some talking birds?" PC Jayawardene was losing the will to live.

"Yes, some birds. Starlings. Are you sure you're a cop? Everyone knows birds don't talk."

Jayawardene considered mentioning parrots, cockatoos and mynah birds. Then she thought better of it in the hope of ending this lunacy quicker, "Right. Starlings, birds. Can you tell me what you witnessed in the restaurant?"

"In the restaurant? I didn't see nothing. I'm calling about the unhygienic bastard starlings *outside* the restaurant. The council won't do anything about them you see and eventually they are going to kill someone. So it's about time the Met stepped up and took over. You know, 'community policing' or whatever it is the Mayor keeps going on about. When he's not banging on about ultra-low emission zones and cameras, obviously."

The incident room hotline had only been open a few hours and already Jayawardene wanted to cry with frustration. Or take up drinking. "I'm afraid this really isn't the right place to raise concerns about birds madam. This incident hotline is trying to gather evidence to help us solve a brutal murder - maybe you have seen something about it on the news?"

"Oh I don't watch the news…"

"You do surprise me madam. Now I'm going to hang up and end this call. Good day."

Immediately the phone began to ring again. It was going to be a very, very long day. PC Jayawardene briefly considered resigning her job, then pushed the 'Connect' button on her phone instead, "Metropolitan Police Incident Room…"

Misadvertised

Chapter Twenty-Two

The operations room was buzzing with energy when Carson and Hewson returned from the crime scene. Woody had been busy, adding new pictures and notes to the murder wall as new intelligence trickled in. The joys of being the most junior member of the team included having to do most of the initial ferret work, chasing down the background info that would help the squad better understand the victims - and hopefully, their killer. Meanwhile, Witz and Evans were both busy on the phones, chasing down anyone who might be connected to the case. The murder wall had expanded significantly, as had the list of potential suspects with verified alibis.

"Damn it," Hewson muttered, two people were dead and the case was going nowhere fast. She knew only too well that murder cases were like marathons. Marathons that dragged on for weeks or months. But with this case it looked like this perp wasn't going to stop - so they didn't *have* weeks to make an arrest.

Carson walked over to the wall, talking as much to himself as the rest of the team, "We have two bodies linked by the Real Rock Restaurant chain. Is this a really weird, highly unlikely coincidence, or has someone been able to establish some kind of connection between the victims yet?"

"As far as we can tell, Nunez and Grabowski didn't know each other, boss," said Witz, "Nunez lived in Greenwich, Grabowski somewhere out in Gospel Oak. They moved in different social circles so we haven't found any cross-over at all yet. It is possible that they may have encountered each other at a works Christmas party or team building event or something, but we're waiting on RRR to confirm."

"If there's no link between vics personally, then it has to be the restaurants," said Evans.

"What about the drugs squad? What did they have to say about Paolo?" Carson was scrambling to cover all angles before they focused all their energy and attention on the restaurant chain as the sole link between victims.

"Nothing boss, sorry. They've never heard of him, said Paolo sounds more like a casual dealer sorting out his mates rather than a real player," Evans explained, "There's no reports of anyone muscling in on the Greenwich territory or new guys slinging large amounts of skunk. However, the drugs squad became super excited about our query and has decided to go and kick in Nicky Ninebar's door tomorrow morning, just in case."

Carson wondered if their routine inter-department query, based on a half-arsed rumour, actually provided anything even close to probable cause for a full-on raid. *Meh, not my problem*, his conscience shrugged.

"Nicky who?"

Evans read from her notebook, "Nicholas Percival Outhwaite, aka Nicky Ninebar. Apparently Greenwich is his turf, so if Paolo's death was related to drug dealing, Mr Outhwaite will know."

Misadvertised

"OK, fine," said Carson, "I want you to tag along on the raid in case anything important comes up. Take the opportunity to talk to Mr Ninebar yourself if you can. And you may as well have the drugs squad check Kirsten as well, see if there is any cross-over there."

Evans nodded and scribbled a quick reminder note in her notebook.

"So at the moment it seems that our vics were just plain unlucky - the killer simply attacked whoever was last on shift," Woody seemed to be thinking out loud, "There's nothing obvious about the choice of victims. This guy seems more interested in drawing attention to his message or his mission or whatever. Like a psycho's manifesto delivered with bodies."

"Pity this wanker couldn't send his grievances in a letter to The Times like in the olden days," Witz complained darkly.

Carson was nodding. They hadn't worked together for long, but his team had proven to be plenty competent. So far, Woody's theory made reasonable sense, "So we're agreed that this is probably the same perp?"

Everyone nodded.

"I've had a look at the Camden restaurant CCTV footage already. The method of entry is different, as is the murder itself, but everything else is the same. Including the careful redressing and disposal of evidence afterwards. It's got to be the same perp - especially as SOCO confirm they haven't found any forensic evidence on or around the body yet," Hewson chipped in.

She called up the footage on the screen mounted on the wall, fast-forwarding through the final moments of

Kirsten Grabowski's short life. She resumed playback as the killer prepared to leave the scene. As before, the man was in no hurry, carefully and methodically placing his hazmat suit, gloves, mask and goggles into a plastic sheet, then rolling the whole bundle into a neat parcel.

"Look," Hewson pinched and zoomed until they could all see the killer's handiwork , "Same double-knot and cable tie arrangement too. It's not a massive clue but it is distinctive."

The secured bundle disappeared into the killer's backpack. Then he simply walked out the back door of the restaurant and disappeared.

"Damn, this guy is *Bad*" said Carson.

"Downright *Dangerous*," Witz sniggered.

"Not you as well," Hewson groaned.

"Anyway, while my partner was glad-handing the local crime lord, I was doing some online research of my own," Evans cut in.

"Oh good Lord," Carson muttered.

"Oh yes," Evans nodded, "The conspiracy forums are in over-drive. The usual nutters have linked the two murders already, and the amateur sleuths are on the case. They have even begun issuing their own online appeals for witnesses and evidence. If we're not careful, these idiots are about to start trampling our case and tainting the witness pool."

"Arse," said Carson, frustrated, "Is there anyone in particular we need to be aware of?"

"Yes, a young guy called 'Sherlock Homes'," Evans saw Carson' raised eyebrow, "Yes, you heard right, H-O-M-E-S, he changed his name by deed poll a few years back

Misadvertised

but forgot to proofread the application form. He might not be great at spelling but he does have good investigative instinct. And he's got form for jeopardising cases - he's been warned several times in the past."

"Brilliant, just what we need. As if this case wasn't hard enough already. Keep an eye on Mr Homes and I'll issue a warning the moment he gets in our way," the DI sighed, "Anyway, I need to speak to AC Chapman, let him know our cases are linked."

"Hey, it's not all bad news Guv," Witz chimed in grinning, "We've had a solid lead from the tip line."

"We have?" Carson was genuinely shocked. The incident room hotline was invariably a drain on resources - and a complete waste of time. For every sensational *Crimewatch* style breakthrough, there were four million calls of zero value. Mostly assorted lunatics making petty complaints in an effort to get their most hated neighbours in trouble with the law.

"Yes," Witz continued, struggling not to grin, "We've had a report of unhygienic killer starlings in the Greenwich area."

The team burst into laughter and Carson rolled his eyes, he had been well and truly suckered. And this kind of tip line nonsense was exactly what he was worried about.

"Sadly that's not the end of the bad news Woody," said Hewson, walking towards the young detective's desk, "From the Greenwich restaurant CCTV it is quite clear that this guy knows exactly where he's going and what he's looking for."

"Which means that he's been there before," his face fell as he arrived at the logical conclusion of this train of thought, "So I'll trawl through footage from the days preceding the attacks to see if we spot anyone suspicious."

"Just keep an eye out for anyone who appears in both restaurants," Hewson added.

Misadvertised

Chapter Twenty-Three

Carson was sat on a hard wooden chair, back against the chilly beige wall, like a naughty child sent to the headmaster's office at school. His brain was humming and he was fidgety, a ball of nervous energy that needed to be directed at catching a killer, not playing politics.

Every now and then the Chief Super's secretary would peer at him like a mole, head popping up over the top of her computer screen, *probably worried I'm stealing stationery or something.* He tried to smile reassuringly at her, but the unfamiliar muscle movements contorted his face into something closer to a snarl, all curled lips and teeth. Much to her relief, the inner office door opened and Chief Superintendent Roger Chapman beckoned Carson in.

Chapman's office was spartan and impersonal, just a cluttered desk with computer, two chairs and a bookcase crammed with paper and foolscap folders. Carson sat in the chair indicated and waited while his boss waddled sideways before sitting his bulging body back down behind his desk. *I wonder why waistline size corresponds to responsibilities?* he thought with a shudder. The senior officer steepled his fingers and raised his bushy grey eyebrows, head inclined slightly forwards like a priest waiting to hear confession.

The DI took this as his cue to speak, "We have an issue Guv."

Chapman nodded sagely, eyes almost closed, "The two murder cases are linked?"

"Uh, yes."

"The press have beaten you to it Carson," Chapman said, pointing lazily at that morning's edition of the Metro newspaper, perched on the edge of his desk. *Real Rock Restaurant Ripper Strikes Again*, screamed the headline, "They've even given him a name."

"Better than the 'Rs Ripper'," said Carson absentmindedly.

"The 'Arse Ripper'?"

"No Guv, the *Rs* Ripper. Real. Rock. Restaurants. R-R-R. Three Rs."

"Oh, right, yes. Hmmmm. Anyway, you already know what I'm about to say," the Chief Super rolled his eyes, "We need this maniac identified and captured as quickly as possible. Police and Crime Commissioner unhappy, residents spooked, London Mayor ranting. Blah blah blah. Sort it out Carson, bring him in. Quick as you can."

"Very good sir," Carson nodded and left. Chapman sucked at motivational speeches and disciplinary dressing downs because he knew his officers were more than competent, they just needed to be able to get on with doing their jobs. That's how you catch bad guys. His refusal to blow events out of proportion to suit the political ambitions of his seniors made Chapman very popular with his juniors.

Carson didn't give a damn about the politics either. He just wanted to get on with his job - and get this Ripper maniac off the streets as quickly as possible.

Misadvertised

Chapter Twenty-Four

Jackson was standing in front of the police barrier on Inverness Street, sunglasses and studded leather jacket in place. His teeth looked unnaturally white set into his Jaffa orange face, framed by his lovingly styled bleach blonde bouffant.

"We're heartbroken that another member of the Real Rock Restaurants family has been tragically slain. Kirsten Grabowski was a beautiful soul, much loved by her colleagues and the community."

"And what would you like to say to the allegation that your restaurant chain is cursed?" the air-headed local TV reporter asked gormlessly.

"Whether you believe in curses or not is a personal matter. All I know is that Real Rock Restaurants have been targeted by a very twisted individual carrying out their own sick personal vendetta. But I'm not afraid. We're not afraid. You hear that Ripper? We're not afraid. Continuing to serve our customers is the best way we know to honour the memory of our fallen colleagues. And I look forward to the moment when the police finally apprehend this... this monster."

"Thank you for your time today," the news anchor turned back to the camera, "That was Max Jackson, CEO of Real Rock Restaurants talking to us from the scene of

another brutal murder here in Camden. Now back to you in the studio."

#

Carson hit the power button and the TV went dead.

"The guy has no shame," Hewson was shocked, "Was he actually trying to cry?"

"Perhaps. But he also has shareholders to satisfy," Carson stroked his chin, "These sorts of crimes can destroy a company you know."

He tapped away at his iPhone for a moment.

"Hmmmmm…."

Chapter Twenty-Five

After spending a few more hours staring at the murder wall, Carson had sent the team home to get some rest. Hewson had politely declined a lift home saying she would catch a bus. In truth, she was grateful for an excuse to avoid listening to another handsfree family domestic. The rest of the team had briefly toyed with the idea of going for a swift half at the Red Lion but eventually decided against; the prospect of rest and sleep won out.

Carson walked towards the car park deep in thought. He was now more convinced than ever that nothing linked the victims other than their place of work. Which meant they were dealing with a mission-driven lunatic - and the Murder Squad would never catch him until they figured out what that mission actually was.

Settling into his car, he briefly considered ringing Eva and trying to reason with her. Maybe try and get her to agree to let him into the house for dinner this evening. He listened to the news headlines instead. When that finished he queued up a classic rock playlist on the in car sound system.

Without really thinking about it he had taken a long detour on the way home, taking him down Inverness Street. He was surprised to see a long queue of people outside on the pavement waiting to get *in* to the RRR.

Weirdos.

Arriving home, the house was in darkness again. Carson racked his memory trying to remember the last time he had actually seen Eva. It took quite a while before he realised he had glimpsed her for a moment that very morning as she darted from the bathroom to their bedroom, dressing gown flapping, wet hair piled into a towel on her head. The memory was so dim and vague, it felt like it could have taken place weeks ago. He missed her even more than he realised.

He staggered dizzily across the lawn and threw himself down onto the camp bed before he fell over, heart hammering against his ribs. Maybe Shaw was right and he should see a doctor. Or maybe he was still just coming to terms with settling back into 'normal' life. Probably just needed some sleep. A lot of sleep.

He picked up the bowl that Eva had left for him, some kind of green Thai curry, judging by the smell. *So thoughtful. God I love that woman - and perhaps, deep down, she still cares for me.*

Carson lay down on the camp bed, staring into the darkness, his imagination painting wild, whirling colours on the black canvas. His mind was racing and his eyes burned, but he could not fall into the embrace of sleep he so desperately needed. So rather than waste the time, he put his wireless earbuds in and queued up Pink Floyd's *Wish You Were Here*.

It had just gone 2am when the shrill ringing of his phone awoke Carson. He had only just slipped into a light doze and was less than happy to wake so soon.

"What?" He barked.

Misadvertised

"Sir, it's Hewson. We have a problem."

Carson was already struggling back into his suit, "I'll pick you up."

Misadvertised

Chapter Twenty-Six

Carson was in a foul mood when he pulled his Audi to a halt outside the Camden Real Rock Restaurant. He leapt out and strode angrily towards the waiting uniformed officer at the door, "I'm very sorry to call you out like this, detective chief inspector…"

Carson growled at the grovelling constable. Hewson shrugged apologetically and followed her boss into the restaurant. Inside, another constable was standing between two extremely angry, aggressive men who were shouting very loudly at each other.

"What is going on here?" Carson thundered, "Who thought it was a good idea to get me out of bed in the middle of the night?"

"You need to ask this idiot," one of the men yelled. It was Jackson, practically frothing at the mouth. He was so angry all pretence of an American accent has disappeared, his broad Brummie elocution coming through loud and clear.

"You did it," the other, younger man shouted back, "You killed Paolo Nunez and Kirsten Grabowski. You're the murderer!"

"*Shut up!*" Carson yelled at the top of his voice. Both men stopped and stared at the DI. For the first time Hewson was able to see the other man. He was tall, thin and

Misadvertised

ridiculously pale, like he never went out in the sunlight. His ashen face was framed by greasy dark hair, gathered back into ponytail that sat under a ridiculous black top hat.

"Why am I here?" Carson demanded.

"Uh Guv," Hewson interrupted, "This is the infamous Mr Homes."

Carson snorted, then asked again, "Why am I here?"

"This, this *idiot*," Jackson pointed at Homes, "Saunters into my restaurant just as we're trying to close up, shouting about me being a murderer."

"That's free speech, man," Homes cut in.

"Shut up," Carson and Hewson said in unison. The DI nodded at the restaurateur to continue.

"Fair enough, free speech, whatever. Just not in *my* restaurant in front of *my* customers. So I asked him to leave."

"He *manhandled* me," Homes whined.

"Last warning. Shut. Up." Carson jabbed his finger at the young man.

"Then the cheeky little bastard tried to steal my glass. So my bar manager called the police."

Carson sighed, "I still have no idea what I am doing here."

"If I may sir," the uniformed constable said meekly, "Mr Jackson asked for you by name."

"You did? Why?"

"Because he's trying to stitch me up," Jackson said, glaring at Homes.

"Mr Jackson," Carson said, gritting his teeth, "The murder squad does not investigate or mediate public order offences or thefts. That is the remit of our uniformed colleagues of whom you have two here already."

"But like me, you *do* investigate murders," Homes broke in again, "And this man here is a murderer."

Jackson lunged for the younger man, but the uniformed constable was faster, shoving him backwards so that he stumbled awkwardly, collapsing at last into a chair.

"Yes, a murderer I say!" Homes was warming to his subject, "I came here tonight to collect samples of his fingerprints to aid my own investigation, hence procuring the man's glass."

Carson grabbed the amateur detective by the collar and steered him to the far side of the restaurant. Meanwhile Hewson spoke to Jackson, hoping to restore some order.

When he thought they were out of earshot, Carson stopped dragging the man and turned to face him, "What do you think you're playing at?"

"Me?" The man asked incredulous, "Why, I'm doing *your* job for you, Detective…?"

Carson ignored the opportunity to share his name, "Do you really think I need advice from a guy who can't spell Sherlock Holmes correctly? Listen you little scrote. *If* you were doing my job, you would have checked his alibi *before* trying to steal his fingerprints. And *if* you had checked his alibi, you would know that Jackson has a rock solid alibi."

"He does?" Again, Homes sounded surprised, "Did you check it?"

"Yes. Now get the hell out of here and don't let me see your face again. If I catch you anywhere near my investigation, I'll have Hewson over there break your kneecaps."

It didn't seem possible, but Homes looked even more pale as Carson delivered his threat. He scuttled for the door and disappeared into the night.

"You're just letting him go?" Jackson yelled.

"Yes Mr Jackson, I am. I'm currently heading up a double murder investigation and I don't have time to complete the paperwork that accompanies a petty theft complaint. Now if you don't mind, I'm going home to get some sleep."

Carson turned on his heel and marched for the door. Hewson nodded a curt, "Good evening" to Jackson and scurried after her boss, worried that he would leave her behind.

Chapter Twenty-Seven

"Well my friends, it's been a busy day for the detectives of the Balls Pond murder squad as their caseload just doubled," Homes frowned insincerely for the camera, "Another body has been discovered, a young woman by the name of Kirsten Grabowski, brutally slain in Camden overnight."

A map popped up on the left of the screen, a bright red dot flashing to show the location of the Inverness Street restaurant. On the right, was a picture of Kirsten, taken from her Facebook profile.

"It appears that poor Kirsten was targeted by the same lunatic individual who murdered her colleague Paolo Nunez. Given the similarities in the cases, it appears that we may be dealing with a serial killer. So from now on, I'll be calling this 'unknown subject', 'The Real Rock Restaurant Ripper'.

A garish full-screen graphic appeared, flashing the new moniker in fluorescent yellow text on a black background.

"My sources claim that this second murder bears the same gruesome hallmarks as Paolo. They also inform me that the murder squad still doesn't have any viable suspects. So I'm going to help them out a little."

"Let's start with means. Who had the *means* to kill these two young people?"

The screen was filled with small passport-sized pictures of all the Real Rock Restaurant employees.

"There's quite a few people there, right? So let's narrow it down by asking who has *motive*."

Immediately, more than half the photos disappeared leaving angry lovers, jealous colleagues and disgruntled customers.

"Still too many. Who had *opportunity*?"

Another handful of images disappeared, leaving Max Jackson, a strange sculpture that appeared to be made out of clay and a large question mark.

"Once we've run through the Three Ms, we're left with Max Jackson, CEO of Real Rock Restaurants, the infamous Beast of Fleet or a third, as yet unknown individual. But I know who my money is on."

Jackson's picture expanded to fill the screen.

"I had the 'pleasure' of meeting Mr Jackson in his Camden restaurant this evening. Having looked into his eyes, his soul, I am more certain than ever that this man is responsible.

"So there you go detectives, I hope this helps. I look forward to hearing about an arrest *very* soon. And for the rest of you, my loyal fans, please hit the Like and Subscribe buttons below. If you have any hot tips or leads, you know where to find me. I'll be back with an up date tomorrow, but until then, sleep safe my friends."

Misadvertised

Chapter Twenty-Eight

Woody was strolling down a street, somewhere on the Greenwich Peninsula he guessed, admiring the angled steel and glass high-rise buildings that stabbed their way towards heaven. The sun glinted off the sharp edges, intensifying the brightness and forcing him to raise his hand to shield his eyes.

For some reason he was dressed in his old PC uniform, sweating under the cumbersome custodian's helmet. Woody had forgotten just how heavy the duty belt and kevlar stab vest were, pulling down on his waist and shoulders. But given the state of London's streets and the surge in knife violence, he wouldn't dream of going on the beat without them. Every other nutter in this city seems to be carrying a blade these days and the Mayor seemed disinterested in trying to solve the issue.

He paused for a moment to shift the weight of his vest and was startled when a large flock of starlings flew along the street. Flying by at head height, he was forced to duck as thousands of the small black birds soared silently past at high speed. He turned and watched as they reached the end of the street, arced towards the sun and then dived back along the road, heading in his direction.

As they approached, he realised that the birds were flying slightly lower, perhaps chest height, and he had to crouch to avoid being struck. The murmuration was not silent this time however, 10,000 pairs of wings whispered, "We're gonna kill you copper."

Woody gasped, *What the hell?* Had he imagined it or did the birds really just threaten him? He'd received plenty of threats while out on the beat, but never from the wildlife. Not even during that shift he did in Newham a few years back.

The starlings repeated the same manoeuvre, reaching the end of the street, curving upwards into the sky then streaking towards the earth, before levelling out at waist level. Woody didn't have time to make it to the shelter of a doorway, so he had to throw himself face down, flat on the ground. Again, the birds passed over whispering, "We're gonna kill you copper."

As he lay on the pavement, a window opened across the street and a woman leaned out. "I warned you," she shouted, "I bloody warned you. I even called your super-duper incident hotline thingy, but you lot ignored me. Serves you right if those little feathered bastards get you. Maybe someone will finally take them seriously. After they kill you." Then seeing the birds were about to begin their next pass along the street, she slammed the window shut again.

This time, the birds were travelling at knee height, no way Woody was going to escape. He grabbed his extendable baton and turned to face the cloud of black feathered demons that hurtled towards him. With one voice, the starlings let loose an ear-splitting cry of fury and Woody realised he would not be able to fight them all. There were just too many of them.

So he turned and ran.

He could sense the tiny bodies getting closer, the murmur of their wings increasing in volume. He could see an open doorway a few yards ahead and he sprinted as fast as his heavy steel toe-capped boots would allow. Too late he spotted the crack in the pavement, his foot catching on the lip, his body falling forwards as the starlings let loose an unearthly scream of pure hate…

THUMP

Woody was still whimpering when he hit the bedroom floor.

Misadvertised

Chapter Twenty-Nine

Evans stretched and yawned. Despite leaving the office early last night she had sat up late mindlessly scrolling social media in the hope of making her brain shutdown - but it hadn't worked. Now, here she was a few hours later, huddled in the back of an unmarked van with the drugs squad, somewhere in the leafy, nice part of Greenwich. The plainclothes officers were all super hyped on adrenaline and caffeine, making them erratic - and a little scary. *Thank God they're not armed*, Evans thought.

Molly Masterson, the DI in charge of the unit had just issued her instructions to the men and turned to Evans, "We'll go in first and secure the suspect. You can wait by the front door until we give the all-clear."

Evans nodded and followed the team as they bundled out of the van towards a fairly average looking semi-detached house with some pretty little flower boxes on the ground floor window sills. The curtains were still drawn and the whole neighbourhood appeared to be slumbering, blissfully unaware of Molly's merry band of stormtroopers and what was about to happen..

"I love this bit," Molly said to Evans. She stepped forward, brushed the door with her knuckles very softly, then whispered, "Police. Open up."

She waited ten seconds, pretending to give the occupant time to act on her instructions. Unsurprisingly, the door did not open.

"Ok lads, off we go," she said with a broad grin.

One of her goons appeared carrying a battering ram, "Aye, aye Guv!" He slammed the heavy steel ram into the door, laughing maniacally as the wood splintered and the hinges squealed and bent under his assault.

The rest of the drugs team surged through the breach, peeling off into each room in the house, all yelling at the top of their voices, "Met Police, stay where you are! Do not move!"

Eventually the sound of thundering footsteps, smashing glass and general mayhem quietened a little and Evans was summoned to the master bedroom upstairs. DI Masterson was standing at the foot of a queen size bed smiling knowingly at a young man propped up on a couple of pillows. Clad in a pair of navy silk pyjamas, the man's face wore a bemused smile under a boyishly tousled mop of thick brown hair.

"Meet Nicholas Percival Outhwaite, aka Nicky Ninebar," Molly said, gesturing at the man.

"You could have just called, DI Masterson," the man said in a slightly bemused tone, "I know you have my number."

"I do indeed," Masterson said with a wink, "But then you know how much I *love* kicking in doors. And Davies was just issued with a new battering ram that he wanted to test out."

"I shall look forward to reading his upcoming Amazon product review then," Nicky said with a smile.

Misadvertised

"Er, good morning Mr Outhwaite. I'm DS Evans," the murder squad detective interrupted, "I'm trying to find out if you know a Paolo Nunez?"

Nicky turned his attention to Evans, flashing her a brilliant smile of genuine warmth. "You're not from round here, are you officer?" then to Masterson, "You have a new squad member, DI Masterson?"

Evans' kicked herself, her stupid countryfied accent had given her away again, "I'm asking the questions, today. Paolo Nunez, do you, *did you* know him?"

Nicky's smile got wider still for a moment, then he shook his head, "The dead guy from the restaurant? No, never met him. Never even *heard* of him until I read about it in the news yesterday."

"Nicky's a bit intelligent see," Molly expanded, "Still reads the daily newspapers."

Nicky gave Evans a comical salute to confirm.

"Well, word is that Paolo was dealing a bit of hash on your turf in Greenwich. Are you ok with new guys chancing their arm in your area?"

Nicky smiled, "I have no idea what you are talking about officer. I don't associate with drug dealers."

Molly snorted but Evans continued unperturbed, "Fine, so where were you on Tuesday night?"

"I met up with some friends, played some cards, chatted, listened to some music."

"He met up with his boys and helped divide up his latest shipment, is what he means," Molly explained.

"I certainly did not do that DI Masterson," Nicky said with a knowing smile.

"Personally, I don't give a toss what you were up to Mr Outhwaite, I just want to know where you were and whether anyone saw you there," Evans tried to bring the discussion back on track.

"We were at the NG Speakeasy, down on Blackwall Lane," Outhwaite answered.

"And afterwards?" Evans scribbled the address into her notebook.

"Afterwards? We were there all night. I left about 6am and came home to get a shower and a few hours of sleep."

"Anyone who can confirm that?"

"Well my friends, obviously. And the bar staff, we kept them busy."

"If you work with Nicholas long enough, you'll soon learn that he's in the NG *every* night," Masterson said to Evans.

Evans threw her notebook and pen onto the bed, "Make a list for me, please. And you can leave Mickey Mouse out."

"Sure thing officer."

"And while you're at it, you can write another list of the people you spent Wednesday night with too."

"Wednesday night?"

"Come on Nicky, it was all over yesterday's papers. Another murder in Camden."

For the first time, Outhwaite looked worried, "Listen, I haven't killed anyone. Not this week, not ever. DI Masterson knows I'm no angel, but murder really isn't part of my business model."

Misadvertised

Evans was inclined to believe him but she needed to be sure, "Just write the lists."

"Do you want my number too, detective?" Nicky asked with a wink.

Despite her best efforts to hide it, Evans felt her cheeks flush slightly.

Misadvertised

Chapter Thirty

Another commute into work, another row between Carson and his wife. Hewson had never met Eva the estranged wife but at times like this she could completely understand why Carson was no longer sleeping in the marital bedroom.

"Give over James," Eva was yelling, "You really think you're going to wrap up a double homicide in time for the two of us to have this weekend away? That you will have recovered your energy and mental balance? Are you assuming that I even want to spend time with you?"

"Yes."

"No. First, you'll need to spend at least another week recovering, sat in a dark room, playing loud rock music, rearranging your bookshelves or making minor pedantic edits to Wikipedia or something."

"Maybe."

"You know I'm right James. Give me a call when the case is closed and we can talk about it then."

Click. Bzzzzzzz. Growl.

Carson cranked up the volume on the car stereo, the opening riff to Black Sabbath's *Paranoid* instantly recognisable as it exploded from the speakers. *Great, old school heavy metal*, thought Hewson as her teeth began to rattle inside her head.

Misadvertised

Speaking of rattling, Carson was visibly shaking, tremors running down his hands into the steering wheel. At first Hewson thought he was drumming along with Bill Ward, tapping the wheel in a show of musical aggression, but the timing was way off. Like Carson was running at 160 beats per minute - or higher.

"Are you ok Guv?" she yelled over an irrationally anxious Ozzy Osbourne.

"What?" He yelled back.

"ARE. YOU. OK?"

Carson reached out and turned the stereo volume down once more, "Yes, I'm fine."

"Really? Only you're shaking like a leaf."

Carson lifted a hand off the steering wheel and held it in front of his face. A puzzled look passed over his face as is he was noticing the tremors for the first time. He placed his hand back on the wheel, grasping so tightly that his knuckles went white.

"Seriously Guv, I can drive if you want. It's no bother."

"I'm *fine*," he growled, eyes fixed ahead, body tensed in an effort to still the shaking.

"You *really* need to see a doctor," Hewson turned towards her own window, muttering, "And a shrink."

Misadvertised

Chapter Thirty-One

Despite the very early start to her morning, Evans had left Nicky Ninebar's house and headed straight over to Camden to meet Witz. They were going to spend the day canvassing homes and businesses in the area together. Hopefully one of them would find another missing detail, a puzzle piece that could point them towards a potential suspect.

Woody had drawn the short straw, trawling through thousands of hours of CCTV collected from the streets surrounding the North Greenwich restaurant. Except there was no straw-drawing contest, it was just part of being the junior squad member, like making rounds of tea for his colleagues and liaising with the officers working the tip line.

As he shuttled back and forth through the footage he realised that none of his team mates seemed to understand just how much 'suspicious' looking activity took place in this part of London at night. CCTV probably hadn't even been invented when Witz started on the job. He finished fast-forwarding through a clip captured by the Mexican chain restaurant next door to the murder scene. Nothing but a bored looking cat and a waiter sneaking a quick spliff on his tea break. He idly wondered if the young man bought his dope from Paolo Nunez.

Misadvertised

Mexican footage complete, he moved on to the next 'tape'. This one was from the faux French café on the other side of the RRR as the team had started calling them.

Trawling through the CCTV recordings was soul destroying. And Woody hadn't even started on the footage collected from the Camden crime scene yet. Worse still, Evans and Witz were sure to have collected even more for him to review when they came back from doing their door to doors around Inverness Street. Video doorbells may be very helpful in solving crimes but some poor bastard, him, had to watch and log it all first.

To make the whole situation worse, Carson insisted on stopping by his desk every twenty minutes to ask if Woody had made any progress yet. Each time he asked, the young detective constable shook his head and felt himself die a little more inside. Was this really why he had slogged his guts out to earn promotion from uniform? Was this really all he could expect as a detective? Would he lose his job when artificial intelligence took over video analysis? At this point, did he even care?

He glanced over at Hewson and shuddered. She was watching Kirsten being choked to death by the hazmat-suited man in slow motion, over and over again, trying to find some detail that would reveal the killer's identity. Maybe he didn't have the worst job on the team after all.

Misadvertised

Chapter Thirty-Two

Day two on the tip line and PC Jayawardene already felt like she had made a massive career mistake. They had received a dozen crank calls from bored school kids, and a few 'nosy neighbour' type reports about stolen bins and parking spaces. Oh, and the starling lunatic, of course. Nothing that had brought the squad closer to catching a killer - or even pointing them in the right direction.

This time when the phone rang, she was much less enthusiastic, "Good morning, Metropolitan Police Incident Room. This is is PC Jayawardene speaking. Please be aware that although you do not need to give your name or number, this call is being recorded. I believe you have some information for the detectives investigating the murder of Paolo Nunez or Kirsten Grabowski?"

"I know who killed the woman in Camden."

"OK sir, could you tell me what you know?" PC Jayawardene could feel the excitement mounting. This might be the break they were waiting for.

"The Beast of the Fleet, you know it?"

"No, I'm not familiar with that name sir, is it a pub?"

"Certainly not. It's a golem."

Pop! Just like that, her excitement evaporated, "Golem? The one from Lord of the Rings?"

Misadvertised

"No, you're thinking of *Gollum*. The Beast of the Fleet is a *golem*. G-O-L-E-M. Golem. It escaped from the synagogue over in Hampstead and entered the tunnels that carry the River Fleet under central London. Now it lives in the sewers under Camden. I saw it myself in the Camden Catacombs."

"I still don't understand sir, are we talking about some kind of animal?"

"No, no, no. It's a bona fide monster. Big bastard, made of clay, possesses superhuman strength. It escaped from its rabbi controller and made its way into the sewers."

"Sir, are you being anti-semitic?"

"Of course not. It's a real thing. The Golem is a real thing. Check it out."

"Right, I'll pass this along to the team and one of our detectives will be in touch if we need any further information. Thanks for your call."

Click.

Misadvertised

Chapter Thirty-Three

Inverness Street itself had been a bust. Evans and Witz had knocked on every door, spoken to every resident and everyone claimed to have seen nothing. Judging by the heavy stench of skunk that hung around the stairwells of the flats above the street, Evans was quite sure that the inhabitants probably couldn't see straight most of the time. They just wanted to complain about the lines of people queuing to get into the Real Rock Restaurant, clogging up the footpath and being a general nuisance.

The two DCs stood surveying the slow-moving queue. Witz pulled his cheap, ill-fitting suit jacket a little tighter and scanned the street for other potential witnesses. A window overlooking the restaurant, a local tramp, covert CCTV, *anything*.

"Word is Carson met our old friend Sherlock last night," Witz sniggered.

"Ha," Evans snorted, "And how did that go?"

"Apparently Mr Homes walked into the Camden restaurant shooting his mouth off, claiming that Max Jackson is the killer. *Then* he tried to fingerprint the bastard."

"What a knobber," Evans laughed.

Witz nodded, "Carson and Hewson got called out to mediate. They probably got home about the time you were leaving to speak to Mr Ninebar."

"Poor bastards," the female DC sympathised, "And my early morning was a complete bust too. I don't think the Drugs Squad ever believed Ninebar was a suspect, they just wanted to kick his door in for fun."

"It's all part of the game," Witz shrugged, "I suppose you need some kind of fun after dealing with the pain and misery caused by drugs and addiction every day."

Yawning, Lisa Evans was pinching and swiping the screen of her smartphone. Still in her late-twenties, she had transferred to the Met after a stellar stint working for Suffolk CID in Beccles. While there she had made national news by helping to solve a major murder case - the first murder in the town for more than 70 years. Evans was attractive, smart and photogenic, so the Metropolitan Police had poached her from the Suffolk force, seeing an opportunity for some positive PR, accusations of sexism be damned.

But while the brass loved her, particularly when it came to promotional photoshoots, the London villains found her countryfied accent to be more hilarious than intimidating. Despite this, everyone agreed that she was a damn good cop. And after a short period of discomfort while she settled in, Evans couldn't imagine trading the city for the sugar beet field of home.

"I think we should check this place out before we jack it in," Evans said, handing her phone to Witz and pointing at the onscreen map to a small alleyway that was located just behind Inverness Street, "Here, there's some more flats and entrances there in Early Mews."

Witz sighed and nodded, following the eager young woman in her flashy blue suit around the corner. What he wouldn't give to have the energy and enthusiasm of youth once more. A small road passed through one of the buildings, and then widened out slightly. The walls of the surrounding buildings absorbed all of the noise of Camden High Street, creating a small oasis of calm. Windows faced out onto the square from every direction, but the place looked deserted.

"I think we can safely say no one back here *heard* anything," said Witz.

"But perhaps they *saw* something," Evans countered, "Look, the rear entrance to the restaurant is over there, between those two buildings."

Sure enough, in between two extensions that had been built over the old 19th century yards behind the Inverness Street properties, there was a sign mounted on the wall of the alley, 'Real Rock Restaurants. Deliveries.' Opposite the alley, a man had come out of one of the stairwells that ran to the upper floors and was getting into a white van parked in a narrow bay.

"Excuse me sir," said Evans, knocking on his van door with one hand, ID in the other. The man wound down his window, "May I ask you a few questions?"

"Sure, if you're quick. I've got to get to work," he definitely wasn't giving off a helpful vibe.

"Do you live around here sir?"

Misadvertised

"Yes, in one of the flats up there," he pointed at the red-brick block that overlooked the square and onto the rear of the Inverness Street properties.

"Were you home the night before last?"

"The night the girl was killed in the restaurant? Some of it. I was working on a job out in Eltham and got home late, maybe 10 o'clockish."

"Did you see anything suspicious?"

"Apart from the cheeky bastard who parked his moped in my space? Nope, nothing."

"Did you see the rider?"

"No, just his bike. I was tired and pissed off, so I moved it against the wall over there."

"Can you tell me anything about the bike? Registration maybe? Or the colour or make?"

"Nah sorry, I wasn't paying attention. It was dark and I was angry, so I just pushed it over and parked my van."

The guy was big and strong. Even seated behind the wheel of his van, Hewson could see that his muscles had muscles rippling under his grubby t-shirt and escaping from his sleeves. She very much doubted he had simply "moved" the errant moped, more likely he threw it at the wall.

"Bugger," Witz muttered in the background.

"OK, thanks for your time, Mr…?"

"Brown."

"Thanks for your time, Mr Brown. Here's my card. Please give me call if you remember anything else."

Brown glanced at the square of card for a moment before tossing it onto his dashboard, along with his collection of receipts and empty crisp packets. The he rolled up his window and drove away through the arch, out onto the main road beyond. Witz and Evans headed for the stairs leading into the flats to continue their door to door enquiries.

Misadvertised

Chapter Thirty-Four

"We're devastated about what happened to Paolo and Kirsten. That's why I'm going to keep doing media appeals until the perpetrator or perpetrators of these horrific crimes is brought to justice."

"And how have these deaths affected the people who work at Real Rock Restaurants?"

"If anything, these tragedies have brought us all closer together. More importantly still, the sense of horror and outrage is bringing the wider community closer together too. Which is the only ray of hope in this terrible situation."

"That was Max Jackson, CEO of Real…"

Carson switched the TV off, "What have you got for me Oaks?"

"Still scrolling and still nothing to report," the young DC sounded despondent, "But I see you made the *Homes on Homicide* show today."

"The what?"

"*Homes on Homicide*. The true crime YouTube channel run by Sherlock Homes," Woody was grinning, "He says he met you, or at least the lead detective, last night and that you confirmed Max Jackson is an official suspect. Oh, and that you threatened to break his ankles if he got in the way of the case."

"Yes we met, no I did not give him my name, nor did I mention suspects and no, I will not break his ankles. I said *Hewson* would do it," Carson growled.

Woody didn't know whether his boss was being serious or not, so he laughed nervously.

"Guv, sorry to make your day even worse, but have you seen this?" Hewson, waved him over to her desk, "I was looking at social media just in case there was something useful in there."

"Bloody hell," said Carson, rolling his eyes, "More like looking for trouble."

"I know, I know, but look at this. The Camden and Greenwich Real Rock Restaurants have become new 'dark tourism' hotspots."

"What?"

"Dark tourism. It's where people visit the scenes of gruesome murders, mass killings, prisons or other unpleasant events and places."

"Like Auschwitz?"

"Well, for some people, yes," she nodded, "But more usually it's places like 25 Cromwell Street in Gloucester or a Ripper walking tour in Whitechapel. Some even visit Marble Arch because it was the site of the Tyburn Tree, rather than for the arch itself."

"Bloody hell," Carson said again, "People really go in for that? I remember a time when people would avoid businesses and places after an event like this for fear it was cursed."

"Yup, but it's nothing new - just larger in scale. Back in the 1600s people were paying to visit the old Bedlam mental asylum to view the patients like it was some kind of zoo. These days there are hundreds of websites dedicated to dark tourism where people give each venue a 'creepiness' rating or simply trade gossip, horror stories and slightly tasteless selfies," Hewson scrolled a little further down the page, "What's really interesting is that RRR is not only listed, but Jackson seems to be milking the notoriety for all he is worth. Look."

She clicked on a picture and it expanded to fill the screen. It looked like one of their official crime scene photos, the body of Kirsten Grabowski sprawled on the floor, head resting on Michael Jackson's red leather jacket. But as he looked closer, Carson noticed something not quite right. First, the restaurant was filled with people. Second, a velvet rope had been strung between several brass poles to create a barrier around the body on the floor. A couple of people contorted themselves backwards over the rope so they could snap selfies with the dead woman.

"Is this one of our pics that has been photoshopped?" He asked.

"No," Hewson shook her head, "It seems that someone on the RRR team has decided to *recreate* the crime scene as the latest addition to his memorabilia collection."

"Bloody hell."

Misadvertised

Chapter Thirty-Five

The murder squad had reassembled for an end-of-day debrief, hoping that a quick information sharing session may spark inspiration, give them a direction in which to focus their efforts.

"So where are we at?" Carson was stood in front of the murder board again, "Let's start with Nicky Ninebar."

"The raid was smooth enough, as was Mr Outhwaite" said Evans, "He seemed perfectly willing to help with our case, but he denied having anything to do with Paolo. Claimed he never even heard of the guy."

Woody took over, "At Evans' request, I called Nicky's mates. Everyone has the same story, cards, music, a few drinks well into the next day. The NG Speakeasy management confirmed Nicky was exactly where he said he was. They're going to send over their CCTV footage from Tuesday and Wednesday to prove it; he was there both nights in the end."

"We never seriously believed this had anything to do with drugs, but..." Carson tailed off into a growl, "Forward the footage on to the Drugs Squad when we're done - maybe there will be something for Molly Masterson to get stuck into."

He moved the mugshot of Nicky Ninebar out of the suspect section of his murder wall, "Hewson, any suggestion your dark tourist weirdos are involved?"

"Not really boss, most seem to be attention-seeking oddbods eager to jump on the next TikTok trend or whatever."

"Tik what?" Carson began, "No stop, I don't actually care. Anything else? Anyone?"

"It may be nothing, but a guy over at Inverness Street reckoned someone had left their bike in his space at the rear of the restaurant…" said Witz.

"Our guy *was* wearing bike leathers and a helmet when he left both Greenwich and Camden," Hewson chimed in.

"Did your witness see the plate? Could they provide a description?"

"The guy said he never saw the rider, just the bike," Evans yawned, "But perhaps we can find it on CCTV in the area?"

Woody groaned, loudly. The problem with London being the most surveilled city in the world is that there is always more bloody CCTV footage to be reviewed.

"Oh yeah, one more thing," Hewson chimed in, "I think we need to organise a team to search the Camden sewers."

"Why?" Carson was already dreading the answer.

"We had another call on the tip line. This guy reckons a killer golem escaped from a synagogue over near Hampstead and it now roams around the tunnels under the streets of London. Called it the 'Beast of Fleet' apparently."

"A golem? Great tip," nodded Carson, "Bung it over to the Marine Policing Unit for follow-up."

"Seriously Guv?"

"No, of course not. DC Oaks can go and check it out."

"What's a golem?" Woody asked, scratching his head.

"Some kind of monster," Carson shrugged, "You can tell us when you find it."

"It's Jewish folklore," Witz interrupted, "A rabbi forms a man-shape from mud, then brings it to life by writing a mystical Hebrew phrase on its head. After that, the golem will do whatever the rabbi commands of it. Including killing people. Apparently they had one in Prague once, tasked with protecting the local Jewish population. It worked great until the golem decided to go on a murderous rampage."

"Good to know, thanks," said Carson, "See what you can find down there Oaks."

"Aw Guv, why me?" Woody groaned.

"Because you keep bitching about the CCTV. I know you're itching to get out in the field. Do some "real" detective legwork."

"Why not send Witz into the darkness? He's Jewish after all."

"What, and that makes me uniquely capable of dealing with golems?" Witz fired back. He wasn't particularly observant, but after enduring years of casual anti-semitism dressed up as 'anti-Zionism', the senior detective was a little touchy about his religious heritage.

Misadvertised

Carson was in no mood for messing around, "Maybe it does. Witz, you take the Beast. Oaks, you're back on CCTV."

Woody and Witz both groaned loudly. Tomorrow was going to suck.

Misadvertised

Chapter Thirty-Six

Carson always looked forward to Friday nights, not least because it meant he wasn't sat in the office or the shed. He could pretend to be a normal human being for a few hours as he hung out with his music quiz team in the Queens Head. The decor was dingy, the beer watery and the service rude, but it still felt like home. Even though he had been gone for two years, it felt like old times when he met up with the guys and he was grateful they had kept a place open on the team for him.

In between rounds, they bantered over pints of bitter, constantly trying to outdo each other with the most obscure facts and trivia they could think of. On the few occasions that Eva had come quizzing with Carson in the past, she had observed that this ritual was simply a modern update of baboons showing off their coloured arses as a way to establish dominance. The DI smiled at the memory before flashing his metaphorical arse at Shaw.

"OK Derek, you're going to have to dig deep for this one," Carson said to his off-duty SOCO colleague, "Which is the only act in history to have a Billboard Hot 100 hit in six consecutive decades?"

Shaw scratched his head. Bob and Bill, the other two team members leaned in. This was a top tier trivia question

Misadvertised

that they would surely use to annoy their disinterested wives when they got home later that night.

"Does this include re-releases?" Shaw was playing for time.

"No, each one was a new release."

Derek could feel three pairs of eyes boring into him. "Elvis?" He asked weakly.

"No," Carson shook his head, "Anyone else want a guess?"

Bob and Bill both shook their heads. Now it was Carson' turn to be eyeballed.

"Well?" Asked Shaw.

"The Isley Brothers. Next round is on you mate."

Bill and Bob laughed as the off-duty SOCO shuffled off to the bar.

An hour later the quiz was over, Carson' team finishing second. Their poor performance on the 'Hits of the 2010s' round had sunk them.

"I'm telling you, we need a younger team member," Bob was saying, "I don't even know what a Dua Lipa is, let alone a Post Malone."

"Maybe you need to figure out how to use that Shazam app like Team Eight," Shaw laughed.

"And there's nothing to stop you inviting a younger, hipper player to join the team," Bill reminded him, "Do you know any young people?"

"You've got kids," Bob countered, "Why don't you invite them?"

"As if they want to go out with a gang of crusty old men like us," Bill sneered, "I can't even get them to *talk* to me at home, let alone be seen in public in my company."

"Good point. Bet they drink those poncey alcopops too," Bob laughed, "See you next week guys."

The two men sauntered off across the pub carpark waving absentmindedly, locked in their discussion about the young people of today. Carson and Shaw were left standing alone in the shadows beside the door.

"So how are you doing?" Shaw asked Carson, staring intently at his face, "Like *really* doing. You were under a long time. Too long. And it sounds like your handler was a little too 'hands off'."

"I'm not going to lie, readjusting has been a nightmare. Some of the stuff I did will haunt me forever. And Eva is still struggling to come to terms with it all."

"Still in the shed then?" Shaw asked with a sad grin.

Carson nodded, "On a rational level she knows that the double-life subterfuge was a necessary part of the job. But emotions aren't always rational, so she's hurting. I'm worried about her. I think she has been more affected by all this than I have."

It was Shaw's turn to nod, "That's very possible. None of the brass really understand what it's like - or the pressure it puts on our loved ones. *You* might get counselling from the Force shrink, but there's no real support for spouses or family. Just make sure you're taking care of yourself - otherwise you won't be able to take care of her. I noticed you're looking a little yellow. Are you eating properly? Drinking too much?"

"We may be having marital difficulties, but Eva is still feeding me, making sure I eat properly," Carson laughed, "She even does me packed lunches. But I'm not feeling great, constantly fidgeting and I can't seem to focus on anything. I think it's just the stress of readjusting to real life. Maybe it's all the bloody paperwork. Maybe it's all the bloody."

Shaw stared at him a moment longer, unconvinced. "We've seen plenty of blood alright. Now go home, get some sleep. And listen, if you need to talk, you know you can trust me," he called over his shoulder as he headed for his car, "Anytime James. Call me anytime."

"Thanks mate."

Misadvertised

Chapter Thirty-Seven

On the other side of town, Evans was making her excuses and trying to leave the Red Lion. She had been up since four am for the raid at Nicky Ninebar's and now it was nearing 11pm. She was tired, she felt sweaty and dirty and Witz was starting to grate on her nerves, constantly moaning about his upcoming trip into the sewers tomorrow. She stood up and began to say her goodbyes.

"Wait, wait, wait. Sit down Evans," Witz said, grabbing at her shirt sleeve "You haven't finished your beer!"

"Come on Charlie, I started the day with a dawn raid and then spent the afternoon pounding the streets of Camden with you. I really need to get some sleep."

"Listen, listen. Woody might have some dirt on Carson."

"Dirt?" She sighed, "Anyone would think you had been drinking Charlie."

She sat back down and folded her arms, "So?"

"So I was thinking, a two year gap in his work record. As I see it, there are only two possible explanations," Woody was suddenly getting very animated, "One, he was seconded to a sensitive unit and his service record is locked to protect his true identity being exposed. Or two, he was in rehab and his record is locked to keep his secret."

"Wow, have you ever considered a career as a detective?" Evans was unimpressed. She got ready to leave again.

"Yeah, but think about it for a minute," Witz took over, "Carson is always hyped, he can't stand still. He's *wired*. Even you country coppers must have seen enough coke heads, stoners and alkies to recognise the signs."

"Clearly doesn't sleep either," Woody added, "Then there's the dizzy spells, tremors, irritability…"

"You make me irritable at the best of times, Woody," said Evans leaning back into her chair. Maybe the guys were onto something.

Misadvertised

Chapter Thirty-Eight

"You're tuned into Homes on Homicide, sponsored tonight by Real Rock Restaurants, bringing you the latest developments in the Ripper investigation."

Homes seemed to be even more animated than usual, arms and hands windmilling with enthusiasm.

"But before we get into the blood and guts, let me mention our sponsor again. As regular viewers will know, I have already named my prime suspect for the murders of Paolo Nunez and Kirsten Grabowski."

A picture of Max Jackson filled the screen.

"This is Max Jackson, CEO of Real Rock Restaurants. Now you may be worried that by sponsoring Homes on Homicide, Mr Jackson is trying to buy my silence. But you'll be pleased to know that we have discussed my position and agreed that I am free to pursue my investigation in any way I see fit - including maintaining Mr Jackson as my prime suspect. Despite this difference of opinion, we are united by the same goal - to catch the killer of Paolo and Kirsten. Even if that ends with Mr Jackson behind bars."

Homes pressed a button on his desk, playing the sound of a prison door slamming shut. Loudly.

"So, with that explanation our of the way, let's get back to the Ripper."

Misadvertised

A title card flashed up on screen, *Meanwhile in Greenwich*.

"Today our friends in the Balls Pond murder squad outsourced some of the heavy work of the Ripper investigation to the Drugs Squad."

The camera cut away to some dramatic smartphone footage of officers kicking Nicky Ninebar's door down. Homes looped the footage a few times for effect, relishing every bang and splinter.

"An impressive show of force, I'm sure you'll agree," Homes grinned at the camera, "But apparently all for nothing. Half an hour later, the lovely Detective Constable Evans left the property empty-handed. No arrests, no evidence bags, no nothing."

"Now my sources indicate the residence in this footage belongs to a mid-level drug dealer which raises the question, are Real Rock Restaurants somehow tied to the drugs trade? A front for shifting narcotics perhaps? Aside from some very low-level skunk dealing in the restaurants, I haven't yet found any links. And certainly nothing serious enough to warrant the murders of two shift managers.

"So what were the police playing at? Chasing down a minor lead? Or maybe just making a big noise to keep London Mayor Carnt quiet?"

A picture of Mayor Carnt sporting devil's horns and a pitchfork flashed up on screen.

"No, he's too busy with traffic cameras to worry about a serial killer terrorising his city," Homes laughed, "Whatever the reason for the raid, it's clear that the police have drawn a blank. Again."

Homes' grin grew even wider, "But that's to be expected when they keep ignoring the actual killer."

Homes winked at the camera before brandishing yet another picture of Jackson at his viewers.

"And that's all I have for you tonight. Please do email me with your tips and leads, and don't forget to hit the subscribe button below. Once again, thanks to our show's sponsors, Real Rock Restaurants. So until tomorrow, sleep safe my friends."

Misadvertised

Chapter Thirty-Nine

Evans is seated in a busy restaurant where faceless waiters wearing white shirts and black bowties float gracefully between the tables, placing vast platefuls of food in front of similarly faceless diners. She scans the room, looking for someone. She's waiting, but for who?

She turns her attention back to her own table only to discover she's no longer alone. A man is sat opposite, his voice is rich and warm, even though he's not speaking real words. But she feels close to him, a fuzzy familiarity that comes from knowing someone deeply. She feels comfortable with him even though she can't make out his face, like it is hidden behind a fogged window. She listens and smiles, enjoying herself and the company, caught up in the moment - it feels like years since she last went on a proper date.

As she sips her cocktail and picks at her entrée, the man's face begins to resolve itself. He's still chattering away but she finally begins to recognise him. Tousled dark hair, nice teeth, boyish good looks, perhaps a hint of a tan. *It's Nicky Ninebar.*

With the realisation comes confusion. Why is she, a copper, sat here having dinner with a known drug dealer? Why does she feel a warm rush of pleasure at he speaks to her? Why is she so confused?

Misadvertised

Laughing easily, Nicky brushes away her concerns and takes her hand, guiding her towards the dance floor. The other faceless patrons dressed in all their finery pirouette past in a blur, just her and Nicky smiling and laughing in their own space and time.

When she wakes, the feeling is still there, an unsettling combination of happiness and disgust and fear. She wasn't sure which was worse, being attracted to a drug dealer or that her dreams were like those of a lovestruck teenager. *What the hell is wrong with me?*

In her half-awake state Evans sincerely hopes she didn't give Nicky Ninebar her card after the raid.

Chapter Forty

"That dickhead Miklos left the door unlocked again," Ivan announced in a thick Ukrainian accent over his shoulder.

"With all the grief going down at Greenwich and Camden? What was he thinking?" Stacey was equally incredulous.

"Knowing Miklos, he wasn't thinking at all."

Ivan didn't blame him. When working the evening shift he had found it hard to concentrate too. A lack of customers meant nothing to do but scroll TikTok on his phone until closing time. That was one of the reasons he had jumped at the chance to take over the day shift - not that it seemed to be any busier.

"And he left the music playing. The neighbours are gonna be pissed," Stacey yelled over the sound of another generic Ed Sheeran hit single blaring from the video screens. There were still a few hours before the restaurant opened, so Stacey headed towards the kitchen to prep ingredients for the lunchtime sitting. Recent experience suggested that most of it would end up in the trash though.

"Can we at least have our own music on until the doors open?" She called out to Ivan who was logging into the computerised cash register behind the bar.

Misadvertised

"You know the rules Stace," he said, shaking his head, "Nothing but the Real Rock Restaurants official playlist. Ever."

"Bollocks," she muttered, "Well turn it down as low as you can then. Like low enough that I can't hear this talentless busker crap any more."

Stacey was just reaching for the door to the kitchen when she was struck a crushing blow from behind.

"Surprised? That's the Godfather of Shock Rock for you," sniggered a muffled voice before striking her again. Hard. Stacey collapsed unconscious, a sickening crack as her head crashed onto the floor.

"Stace? Are you alright?" Ivan called out, "Stacey?"

Receiving no reply, he made his way towards the kitchen. As he rounded the corner of the bar, he saw a figure dressed head to toe in a coverall suit, like those you see on crime drama shows. Stacey lay sprawled on the floor, a man standing over her prone body. He was brandishing a polished black wooden cane in his blue plastic gloved hand, preparing to bring it down on her head.

Ivan broke into a sprint, diving through the air and crashing into the man's midriff. The attacker went down under Ivan's attack, both men falling backwards through the swing door to the kitchen. As they hit the floor, the attacker managed to roll on top of Ivan, pinning him in place. The cane had spun away in the fall, so the man resorted to punching Ivan repeatedly in the face. The Ukrainian heard his nose splinter, felt the warm blood running down his cheeks, saw the man stand up and retrieve the cane. Then everything went black.

Misadvertised

Chapter Forty-One

Despite being relatively early on a Saturday morning, a small crowd of excited onlookers had already gathered outside the Real Rock Restaurant in Soho. Some looked like all-night revellers who were staggering their way home from a rager. Others were clearly more invested, dark tourist weirdos who had picked up the digital rumours online, hoping to glimpse some real life gore. In the middle of them all, jostling between the television journalists, Sherlock Homes was conspicuous, his battered top hat standing high above the surrounding crowd. He held his smartphone aloft defiantly, filming the police as they rushed to-and-fro, trying to secure the scene. Carson was pleased to see Homes pale slightly when he caught sight of Hewson.

"Deep breath Hewson," Carson said, pushing the glass door open, onto the scene of another bloodbath.

"Not again," the DS groaned following Carson into yet another real-life version of a 1980s video nasty. As before, the walls, floor, furniture were painted crimson. If anything, there was even more blood than there had been at Greenwich. But when she saw there were two bodies this time, it was obvious why.

"Bloody hell," she said.

Misadvertised

"If Hell is bloody, this is what I imagine it will be like," Carson agreed.

The two corpses sat upright, tied to chairs, opposite each other across a table. Both had been battered severely around the face and head.

"*Welcome to My Nightmare*. No offence, but I was hoping not to see you until next week under much happier circumstances," Shaw appeared from further back in the restaurant. He was impossibly cheerful given the horrific tableau that greeted them.

"I guess this proves that not *Only Women Bleed*," Carson quipped, "Thank God Alice Cooper doesn't donate his guillotines to outlets like this, eh?" He wandered off into the building leaving Shaw to give Hewson a quick run-down.

"A guillotine would have been much faster and more humane than this. Two vics, obviously. One male, one female," Shaw pointed at each corpse in turn, "They are believed to be Ivan Yushenko, day shift manager and Stacey Kyle, head chef."

He turned and gestured to a distraught young man waiting outside in the street, "They were found by the head waiter when he arrived to start his shift."

"Obviously we'll have to wait for the post mortem to be sure, but I think we can safely say cause of death for both vics is blunt force trauma. The murder weapon, an Alice Cooper prop cane, was left on the table, there, along with a microphone used by Billy Idol."

Hewson moved in for a closer look. A lack of nausea made her worried that she may be becoming accustomed to brutal slayings.

"What's the microphone all about?"

"Not sure actually. Oh, hold on. Oh…" Shaw's eyes widened above his mask as he examined the bloody mess which had once been Ivan's head, "I have a face without eyes."

"And I have *Eyes Without a Face*," Carson called back from the other side of the room.

Misadvertised

Chapter Forty-Two

Carson and Hewson weren't the only ones facing a sensory onslaught. Witz waited at the bottom of a dank stairwell while an engineer, Barry, from Camden Borough Council unlocked a heavy, rusted metal door. He was dressed in waist-high waders, yellow hard hat and a bright orange high-viz jacket, loaned by his colleagues from the River Police.

As the door swung open a rush of foul air burst forth, the stench causing Witz to retch and choke.

"Don't worry mate, take a few deep breaths and you'll get used to it. Ollyfactory Disinfectionisation or summat." Barry advised him. Bent double, Witz continued to cough and retch. The smell was so bad the DS had no trouble believing that Barry had just opened a portal into the very depths of Hell itself. Or perhaps its bowels.

"Right, let's get this done then, shall we?" The engineer said, strolling into the darkness. Witz followed behind as they descended down more stairs, the air as thick as the darkness. He swept his flashlight across the brick walls, pausing for a moment to admire the vaulted brickwork tunnels that carried the subterranean River Fleet under London's streets.

Eventually they reached the bottom of the stairs where a stream rushed by, ripples twinkling under their flashlights.

"So what are we down here for again?" Barry asked.

"'The Beast of Fleet'," Witz rolled his eyes.

"Ah yes, The Beast," the man sounded like he was regularly asked to help track clay monsters from Jewish folklore, "This way then."

The short, thin engineer jumped straight into the stinking water and Witz was relieved to see it was only knee deep. Barry didn't wait for the detective, immediately setting off downstream, the current creating small waves around his legs. Witz climbed gingerly into putrid blend of water and sewerage, eager to catch up with the engineer before he was left alone in the darkness. He didn't believe in golems, but he also didn't want to be stranded down here. And he definitely didn't want to think about what was swirling around his shins.

"Where are we going?" Witz shouted over the sound of rushing water.

"The Catacombs," the engineer yelled back, "That's where we're most likely to find him."

Barry sounded as if he not only believed in the golem, but that he had possibly even seen the golem himself. *Crazy troglodyte*, Witz thought to himself.

They continued pushing upstream, through large arches and along tunnels. Every now and then they would pass other smaller passageways branching off to the side, bricked portals to who knows where. It was like an amazing maze, an impressive feat of Victorian engineering, monumental in scale, ingenuity and appearance.

Misadvertised

Particularly when most Londoners didn't know it was there, would never get to see it.

It was hard to judge distances in the dark, but Witz thought they had walked about half a mile when the engineer stopped. He pointed ahead to an iron ladder affixed to the wall, then ran his torch up its length to where it disappeared into a hole in the roof.

"I guess we're going up there then," the detective muttered to himself. Barry was waiting at the bottom, shuffling from foot to foot, so Witz assumed he was climbing first. He put his foot on the bottom rung and hauled himself hand over hand, passing through the curved ceiling of the tunnel and into a large space beyond. It was much quieter above the water and the echoes of his movements suggested he was in a giant chamber. His torch danced along the walls, picking out more vaulted brickwork, arches disappearing far off into the darkness.

"Boo!" Barry yelled, his head poking out from the floor. Witz jumped and swore, his guts turning to liquid.

"Ha ha, just my little joke," the engineer chortled to himself. Witz had a good mind to kick the man in the head, make him fall into the stream of stinking brown water below. Serve him right. Instead he turned away, pretending to admire the stained and blackened bricks that surrounded them on all sides. "Do that again and I will hit you," Witz growled.

"Anyway, welcome to the Camden Catacombs," Barry was grinning, holding his arms wide and gesturing to the echoing space around them.

"So where are the bodies?" Witz asked, puzzled.

'Ah yes, well," Barry muttered, "There aren't any."

Misadvertised

"No bodies? Where did they go?"

"There never were any bodies down here. The Catacombs is a nickname made up to scare the local kids. It's actually just a bunch of tunnels and storage areas under Camden Market. They used to walk horses along the tunnels between the old station and the canal. And there are some even bigger chambers where there were massive engines used to pull heavy trains between Euston Station and Camden Town. A lot of it is flooded now though..."

Witz sensed a full-blown history lesson was about to start, "Right, great. So what about The Beast. Where do we find him?"

"He's bound to be round here somewhere," Barry shrugged, "Let's split up and meet back here in 15 minutes."

"Have you never seen a horror movie, Barry?"

"Yes?" Barry looked at him quizzically, "Why?"

Witz shook his head, "No reason."

Barry shrugged again, then shuffled off under a large brick arch. Witz watched the circle of light getting smaller as the man walked away, then he turned and headed in the opposite direction. After a few hundred metres he had completely lost sight of Barry's torch.

Witz continued walking, sweeping his flashlight beam from side to side. There was nothing much to see - piles of old wood and ropes, thousands of ancient footsteps rushing here and there through the dust. Occasionally he caught the glimmer of beady eyes lurking in the shadows, *plague-ridden rats no doubt*. Witz was more than a little creeped out as the blackness got thicker, closing in on him from all sides.

Misadvertised

He was about to give up and head back when he caught sight of something off to the right, up against the wall. A stack of carrier bags, blankets, food wrappers, rubbish. He edged closer - it was a shelter of some kind. Someone was living down here.

He crept closer and pulled at a corner of the makeshift tent to reveal an equally makeshift sleeping space beyond. He was desperately relieved to find the bed unoccupied, the giant clay golem was nowhere to be seen. But what caught his attention was the distinctive black and red backpack resting on top of a filthy, blue sleeping bag. He pulled on a pair of latex gloves and carefully unzipped the bag. It was empty and wet, soaked through with sewerage. *Arse.* Maybe the forensics lab could pull some trace off it, but he doubted it.

He was just standing up, when he felt a shadow behind him, freezing his blood. Witz span round in fear.

"Boo!" Barry yelled.

Witz continued to turn, his arm whipping around in arc. The movement took a fraction of a second, but time seemed to telescope and slow as he moved. He watched in horror as his flashlight smashed against Barry's temple, bulb shattering. There was a spray of blood and the man crumpled to the floor with a gurgling groan. Barry's own torch skittered crazily across the floor and Witz scampered after it, afraid of being left alone in the dark.

He fell to his knees and grabbed the torch, turning the beam to point at Barry's prone form. The man's eyes stared sightlessly into the darkness above, his head twisted at a crazy, uncomfortable angle. Witz gagged. Barry was dead.

Misadvertised

"I told you, I *told* you," Witz yelled at the body, giving Barry's corpse a swift kick for good measure, "You stupid, stupid idiot."

He began to pace up and down in front of the body and the makeshift tent, mind in overdrive. *Call it in. And say what?* Even if he could prove it was an accident, Witz's career was over, he was going to prison for manslaughter. *Shit, shit, shit.*

"What are you going to do Witz?" He asked himself panicked, "Come on, *think.*"

He bent down over Barry's body and felt for a pulse. Nope, he was definitely dead. *Shit, shit, shit.*

He hadn't meant to kill Barry, it was an accident. So it didn't really matter *how* the accident had happened, he reasoned to himself. Either way, Barry wasn't going home for dinner tonight, so why should he have to take the fall for the man's stupidity? Why should he lose everything because the stupid bastard wanted a laugh at his expense?

"You're a decorated officer, Witz," he yelled at himself, "You can't just lose all that because of a mistake. He brought this on himself."

Witz stopped pacing and came to a decision. He wasn't to blame and he wasn't going to take the blame either. It was an accident. He picked up the stinking, empty backpack from the tent and slung it over his shoulder. Then he grabbed Barry's ankles, dragging him back through the darkened archways towards the ladder they had climbed. It seemed to take forever, but eventually he found the opening in the floor, the sound and stench of the rushing sewerage below guiding him through the dancing shadows cast by his torch.

Witz could feel the perspiration dripping off his face, rivulets of sweat running under his shirt and trousers, fabric sticking uncomfortably to his skin. He dropped Barry on the ground, then hurled the rucksack into the hole, relieved to hear a distant splash. Feeling faint and exhausted, Witz rested for a moment, struggling to catch his breath, giving himself one last chance to back out of this crazy course of action.

Finally he set his jaw, pushing Barry through the hole in the floor. There was a loud metallic clang as he bounced off the metal ladder, then a loud splash as the River Fleet carried Barry's body away into the stinking darkness.

Misadvertised

Chapter Forty-Three

Back in Soho, Hewson had excused herself to vomit loud and long out in the street. Despite the acid burn in her throat she was relieved that she was not yet hardened to horror.

"She's had a bit of a *Shock to the System*," Carson noted with a wink. He and Shaw stared at the TV. Onscreen, Ed Sheeran's enormous ginger head looked at them mournfully. Two bloodied eyes - Ivan's - had been stuck to the glass, staring back at the investigators.

"Do you think he used the microphone to gouge the guy's eyes out?" Carson asked.

"It's the most stupid choice of implement, one of their famous RRR steak knives would have been a much more suitable tool," Shaw nodded, "But I guess this maniac has a message they want us to 'see' so yes, I think he did use a microphone for the enucleation."

He pointed at the wall where the killer had smeared a message in blood on the wall: *NO! WHAT PART OF THE MESSAGE DO YOU NOT UNDERSTAND?*

"He's also written a '*YES!*' under the empty Billy Idol and Alice Cooper display cases," Carson noted.

"Bloody hell," Shaw muttered, "I guess you *Don't Need a Gun* to make a statement."

"Full marks for effort," Carson nodded, "But but that one was poor. Anyway, photograph everything, bag it up and send me over your preliminaries," Carson said, heading for the door.

"You're not looking any better," Shaw called after him, "Your skin is still yellow. And I can see you're having problems with your balance too. Get yourself to the doctor James."

"Yeah I will," Carson called back, "Maybe."

He had his hand on the front door handle when there was an unearthly gurgling sound from one of the corpses.

"What the f...?" Hewson screamed.

"Bloody hell, it's Stacey, she's still alive," Shaw shouted. He scrabbled to cut the cable ties securing her to the chair, "Call an ambulance. Now!"

Carson rushed to help the SOCO free the woman, laying her gently on the floor. Stacey continued to gurgle and choke while Hewson frantically dialled 999.

"Lay her on her side, otherwise she's going to choke," Shaw was still shouting. They rolled the woman's body as tenderly as possible, and Carson took off his jacket, using it to try and staunch her bleeding. The non-absorbent material was useless, like trying to soak up blood with clingfilm.

"The ambulance is three minutes out," Hewson yelled.

Stacey began to struggle against the men, her battered and torn face making horrific animalistic noises, a howl of pain that crescendoed in a scream of pain, a sound so awful that Hewson's blood froze, a stabbing fear in her gut. But the more Stacey scrambled, the worse the bleeding got. Her breathing was getting shallower, slower, more laboured.

Her limbs flailed and slipped in the pool of her own blood that was spreading across the floor. Shaw and Carson struggled to stop her moving.

"Hold on Stacey," Carson begged, "Please hold on. Just a few more minutes. Help is coming."

But it was too late. She was gone.

Chapter Forty-Four

Driving away from Soho, Carson allowed Hewson to sit in shocked silence. Hewson tried not to notice Carson was still covered in Stacey's blood, so fresh that it was seeping into the upholstery of his seat and creating a sticky mess on the steering wheel. Instead she stared sightlessly out the window as the grey streets of London passed by in a blur, hoping to forget that awful cry of pain and despair escaping from Stacey's battered body.

Eventually Carson spoke, "I have an idea what the killer is trying to say."

Hewson nodded that he should go on, anything to try and push the memory of Stacey's minced-beef face away for a few minutes.

"I think it's to do with music. I think the killer is punishing the Real Rock Restaurant chain for playing pop music."

Hewson turned to face him, "No, that's absolutely insane. No one kills anyone over music."

"Are you sure about that? Have your grandparents ever told you about the mods and the rockers and their seaside brawls in the 1960s? Maybe you could read up on Emperor Charlemagne's decree to Roman Catholic priests that Gregorian chant be the official church liturgy - on pain of death? Charles Manson's homicidal mania inspired by The Beatles?"

Hewson shook her head, "These all sound like excuses."

"Perhaps, but the fact that perpetrators are willing to blame music simply emphasis just how powerful it really is. You could always drop by the Met Gang Unit and ask them for some anecdotal evidence about the correlation between knife crime and drill music?"

"Good point," she turned to stare out the window once more.

Carson blinked back his tiredness and hit speed dial on his handsfree, "Masterson? It's Carson. I have two more names to run past you."

"Hi James, I'm fine. How are you?" Molly asked sarcastically.

"Ha ha," he laughed robotically, "Ivan Yushenko or Stacey Kyle?"

"Nope. Never heard of them."

"Like you'd never heard of Paolo Nunez?"

"Yes," Masterson sighed, "Exactly like Paolo Nunez who we had never heard of."

"Fine." Carson hung up.

"I know it's been a crappy day, but do you understand even the basics of politeness, Guv?" Hewson asked, "Like friendly small talk? Or even a simple 'thank you'?"

"Yes. No. I don't know," Carson shrugged, "I'm busy, she's busy. Does it really matter?"

So that was a no then. Hewson decided to move on, "I'll ask Witz to get started on alibis and background checks for the Soho staff."

Carson nodded, "They won't find anything, but we need to go through the motions anyway. Tell him to delegate the legwork to uniform."

He punched some numbers on the car's entertainment system display.

"Max Jackson speaking," the fake US accent was still grating.

"Jackson, this is DI Carson."

"Yes, detective. What..?"

Carson cut him off, "You need to close your restaurants until we catch this guy."

"Sorry detective, no can do. Our public want, *need,* us to be open at this difficult time."

"Cut the crap Jackson, I'm not one of your idiot investors," Carson snarled, "Three people have been murdered and it seems highly likely - *almost inevitable* - that the killer will strike again. For the safety of your employees and 'your public' you need to shut them down. All of them. Immediately."

"As I said, no can do. Goodbye." Jackson cut the call.

"What a wanker," said Hewson, "Is there anything we can do?"

"No idea. I'll kick it up to Chapman. Maybe his friend the Mayor can do something," he said with a wicked grin that looked all the more evil given the amount of blood he had smeared all over him.

Misadvertised

Chapter Forty-Five

"We love everyone and we serve everyone," Max Jackson was saying, *"Our staff put their souls, put their lives, into providing the best experience for customers at Real Rock Restaurants. We're one global family and it's terrifying to think that one deranged individual is seeking to destroy that culture.*

"But we're not going anywhere. We won't be scared into closing. We'll be open tonight, and every night, for as long as our customers, our family, wants.

"Please join us tonight at your nearest Real Rock Restaurant tonight as we stand against hate."

"That was Max Jackson, CEO of Real Rock Restaurants, scene of four horrific murders this week. And in other news..."

Misadvertised

Chapter Forty-Six

Carson had taken quite some time trying to wash Stacey's blood off his hands and face - and his memory. His clothes were ruined too, forcing him to borrow a spare shirt and trousers from Woody's locker, both of which were a little too small and tight for comfort.

Half an hour later, he was in front of the murder wall again. Almost nothing had changed apart from the word 'motorcycle?' And two new murder victims.

"Uniform have spoken to the Soho staff and everyone has alibis for this morning, Guv," Evans was saying, "I'm about to double-check the details but there's no discrepancies so far. The other staff weren't due in for at least an hour after Yushenko and Kyle arrived - most hadn't even got out of bed in fact."

"There have to be some benefits to a job on minimum wage, I guess," Carson noted.

"Similarly, background checks don't throw up anything too concerning," Evans chipped in, "One caution for drunk and disorderly, two outstanding parking tickets and an incident of B&E five years ago - charges dropped."

"It would be quite a step up from breaking and entering to four counts of murder. Any mental health angles to consider?" Hewson asked, looking for an alternative approach, "Anyone ever sectioned for instance?"

"Nothing flagged up," said Evans, "but I will double-check."

"Witz, how did you get on with the Beast of Fleet?"

Staring out the window, Witz didn't seem to hear.

"Witz?" Carson clicked his fingers at the DS like he would a disobedient dog.

"Sorry Guv, what?"

"The Beast, the Golem. Did you find anything?"

"Spent a couple of hours poking around down there, it's like a rabbit warren, only darker. I'm not saying there's nothing down there, but if there's a golem, we didn't find it. Complete bust, sorry Guv."

"I'm impressed that you are leaving the possibility of a golem open for now. But it's a shame the clay monster couldn't give us an elimination statement," Carson turned his attention to Oaks, "Any joy on the CCTV, Woody?"

"Oh endless joy sir, unicorns and daffodils and rainbows," said Woody sarcastically, "You would not believe how much I look forward to coming into the office each morning. I just can't wait to…"

"Oaks," Carson growled, "What have you got?"

Woody jumped, "Two things Guv. First, Homes has uploaded a rather juicy video of DS Hewson talking loudly to a potted plant outside the Soho restaurant. She has knocked you off the front page of *Homes on Homicide* blog, sir."

"What?" Carson had no idea what Woody was talking about, "Talking to plants? On that idiot's internet TV show?"

"Oh, please no." Hewson buried her head in her hands, "Tell me he didn't."

"Yes, he did," Woody was grinning, "At this rate of clicks, you're on course to be his most popular video of all time."

Hewson groaned, "My Mum watches Homes on Homicide."

"She will be so proud! You're internet famous!"

"Oho, that's bad," Witz was laughing from behind his own screen.

"Bloody hell Hewson, what did you eat for breakfast?" Evans was now giggling too.

"I can't stop watching," Witz was crying, turning his screen so Carson could see Hewson chundering violently into a potted plant outside the Soho restaurant.

"If we're quite done with the vomiting videos, could we please get back to the slightly-more-important issue of the four murders we are supposed to be investigating?" Carson snapped, "Oaks! Tell me the second thing you found was actually relevant to the case?"

"Yes, sorry Guv," Woody tried to choke down his laughter, "I found a few glimpses of a motorbike that seems to appear in both Greenwich and Camden. I'm fairly sure it's the same make and model each time, but I'm having trouble reading the plates to confirm. IT forensics are trying to clean up the best of the stills and running one of their magic automated recognition algorithms across the images for me."

He handed a printout to Carson who stared at it for a moment. "Are you sure that's even a motorbike?" He asked as he pinned the pixellated blob to the murder wall, next to where he had carefully scrawled 'motorcycle?' previously. He carefully erased the question mark.

"There's one other thing I noticed Guv," Woody piped up again, "While I was scanning through the footage from Greenwich and Camden I realised we had missed something."

"Which is…?"

"There were other people in the restaurant."

"What? Who?"

"The delivery drivers."

There was silence for a moment.

"Bloody hell," Hewson mumbled. They had all missed it, the whole squad.

"Think about it," Woody was warming up now, "The delivery drivers are invisible and ignored, pretty much free to wander the restaurant floor without anyone paying them any attention - they are just part of the furniture. So when we asked the staff who was on shift, they told us the names of the *employees*. But the delivery guys work freelance via their apps. I doubt the triple-R staff even notice the same drivers twice, let alone know their names."

"*Bloody hell*," Hewson said, a lot louder this time.

"OK, Evans I want you back at Inverness Street tomorrow morning. Speak to the van driver and see if you can get a description of the bike and its rider," Carson said.

"Might be worth checking to see if he has any dash cam footage too," Hewson added.

"As for you Witz, I need you to get onto the food delivery app operators and have them track down all the riders who were working Greenwich, Camden or Soho. Better still, save us some time and find out if any of them were making collections at all three venues on the nights in question."

Witz nodded.

"And seeing as you've done such a sterling job so far Oaks, you can continue with the CCTV," Carson finished up, "I'm going to call Real Rock Restaurants HQ and firmly insist that is they refuse to shut down, they *must* switch to a rock-only soundtrack at all of their venues for the foreseeable future. Then I'm going to do a drive-by to make sure head office have passed on the message. As for the rest of you, go home and get some sleep. Hopefully we won't be waking up to any new bodies in the morning."

Chapter Forty-Seven

"Good evening, Metropolitan Police Incident Room. This is is PC Jayawardene speaking. This call is being recorded, but you do not have to give your name if you do not wish to do so and everything you say will be held in strictest confidence. What can you tell me?"

"This is Muriel Spence calling. I believe the man you are looking for is called David Reid and he lives at 21 Darville Road in Hackney."

The caller was clearly an elderly woman. Jayawardene scribbled the name 'David Reid' on her dogeared notepad.

"You seem very certain Muriel. Can I ask why you think Mr Reid may be the man we're looking for?"

"Well, he's very polite and very, very quiet. Keeps himself to himself you see."

"OK Muriel," Jayawardene tried not to sigh audibly, "Anything else?"

"Well on TV they always say it is the nice quiet ones. They are the ones that no one suspects. That's how I know Mr Reid is the killer you're looking for."

PC Jayawardene had to admit she was somewhat suspicious. What kind of a weirdo was quiet and polite these days in London? "Is there anything else you can tell me about Mr Reid? Anything else to help our detectives?"

"Anything else? The man has all the traits of a psychopathic serial killer. He's quiet, patient, kind, not a busybody..."

"Perhaps," Jayawardene tried not to sound like she was agreeing, "I will pass this information to the murder squad detectives and someone will be in touch to follow up. Thank you for your call Muriel, bye bye."

Click.

Misadvertised

Chapter Forty-Eight

Carson was now used to see crowds of gawkers gathering outside each Real Rock Restaurant, weirdos queuing in the dark, waiting for their turn to sit on a chair that may have once been used by a victim - or a serial killer. He was also quite used to elbowing his way through the queue, flashing his badge angrily at anyone who dared question this breach of etiquette.

With a final flourish of his warrant card for the benefit of the gorilla-shaped security guard on the door, Carson gained entrance to the Soho restaurant. Every table was full, diners laughing and shouting or singing along to AC/DC playing Highway to Hell on the video walls. As with the other restaurants, Max Jackson had created an all-new display to remember the murder victims, topped by a replica of the now-infamous Alice Cooper baton. The real one was still logged in evidence at the forensics lab.

It was hard to believe this was the same place where two people had been battered to death less than 24 hours earlier. Thankfully Jackson had decided not to recreate the blood spray - his decorators and cleaners had actually done a stellar job of removing red stains from the floor, walls and ceiling. AC/DC came to an end and Led Zeppelin took their place onscreen, instructing the diners they needed a *Whole Lotta Love*. Carson nodded appreciatively.

He spotted the RRR CEO at the bar, again surrounded by a gang of groupies hanging on his every word. No doubt more of those lunatics from the dark tourism forums, basking in his infamy. The sort of desperately lovestruck weirdos who marry serial killer lifers.

Behind Jackson stood a huddle of dead-eyed delivery drivers carrying bags shaped like huge fluorescent orange cubes. Each stared at their smartphones while they waited for the kitchen to prepare the orders that needed to be delivered to hungry customers sat at home. One or two of the riders hadn't even bothered to remove their helmets, *Maybe they're not rock fans.*

Carson caught Jackson's eye and nodded an acknowledgement, noting the smug look of satisfaction on the restaurateur's face. Jackson was enjoying himself, basking in the attention and infamy, giving his audience a vicarious thrill through his proximity to each of the victims. Disgusted and disturbed, Carson walked back out the front door as the thrumming bass guitar intro of *Keep the Faith* came thundering over the sound system.

As he walked back to the car, Carson fished his smartphone out of his pocket, "Hewson," he launched in as soon as his DS answered the phone, "Did we ever check Jackson's alibi?"

"Yes, I'm having a great evening Guv, thanks for asking. No, no of course you're not interrupting anything important," she replied sarcastically, then after a beat, "No, we haven't yet managed to get hold of the therapist. Dr Jenkins works some funny hours apparently."

"Fine, then we need to check him out tomorrow."

"Fine," said Hewson, "assuming we can get hold of him."

But Carson was already gone.

As he walked back to his car, he stumbled and nearly collapsed. Feeling faint, he leaned against a nearby wall for a few minutes, struggling to catch his breath - and hoping the pain in his chest was not the onset of something serious. He rested his forehead on the bricks, trying to cool the raging fire in his chest.

Eventually the feeling passed and he was able to drive himself back to the shed. Perhaps Shaw was right and he really did need to get himself checked out.

Misadvertised

Chapter Forty-Nine

"As I see it, *if* we're right about Carson having a problem, we have three options," Woody took a mouthful of beer and made a face, then started counting on his fingers, "One, someone contacts professional standards anonymously and let them deal with it. Two, someone has an informal chat with Chapman. Three, we do nothing until we've spoken to Hewson about what is going on."

"There is a fourth," Evans added.

"Oh yeah? What?"

"We take the grown up option. One of us speaks to Carson himself."

"Yeah," Woody shook his head, "But no."

"What do you say Witz?" Evans nudged her partner who was staring off into space, "Earth to Charlie. What's going on with you tonight, mate?"

"Long day in the dark, wet and stinking of excrement, chasing an ancient Jewish myth because Woody was too frightened to go down in the tunnels. Worried he was going to meet a killer clay man," he muttered, "I'm too old for that kind of crap."

Evans sensed something was wrong but she couldn't put her finger on it. She had never had to force Witz into the pub after work, he practically lived in the Red Lion, but tonight he had tried to cry off. Very, *very* weird.

Woody ignored the dig. Instead he reeled through their four suggestions again, "So which would you suggest?"

Witz lifted his eyes slowly from his glass, his brain felt like it was full of treacle. "OK," he sighed, "I'm not going anywhere near professional standards. Once you involve those bastards, they get into everything. They'll be all over Carson *and* us, even if we haven't done anything wrong. I don't know Hewson well enough to have this kind of chat with her. And there's no way I'm going to confront the Guv, even if he has triggered my hunch."

Despite being as mythical as a Golem, all Met Police officers have an unshakeable belief in the Copper's Hunch and its infallibility. Witz was no different, if his hunch was triggered, he was certain something was amiss - and its cause.

"So that leaves Chapman," Woody summarised.

"Well you've worked with him for years," Evans nodded, "I nominate you Charlie."

"Pffffft, no thanks," Witz shook his head, "You're his golden girl. *You* should speak to him."

The argument went to-and-fro for bit longer. Eventually Evans and Woody ganged up on the older DS, "You invoked your hunch, so you're nominated Charlie. You can speak to Chapman tomorrow."

Damn.

Misadvertised

Chapter Fifty

"Welcome to episode #2976 of the Homes on Homicide show, sponsored by Real Rock Restaurants. Before we get started, I would like to extend my condolences to the families of Ivan Yushenko and Stacey Kyle who were tragically murdered this morning by the Real Rock Restaurants Ripper. Tragically both were killed in broad daylight - and yet *no-one* saw anything. Perhaps most shocking of all, Ivan and Stacey brings the death toll to four, highlighting the astonishing incompetence of the Met Police.

"And I may talk more about that incompetence shortly. However, tonight we have a guest on Homes on Homicide," the camera angle widened, to reveal another man sat on the opposite side of a low metal desk, "I'd like to introduce Mr Max Jackson, CEO of Real Rock Restaurants and my prime suspect in these brutal slaying. Welcome Mr Jackson."

Homes pressed a button, canned applause and whistling played loudly for a moment.

"Max, please," Jackson smiled briefly, then adopted a somber voice, even removing his trademark sunglasses, "Before we go any further, I would once again like to extend my sincerest condolences to the family and friends of Paolo Nunez, Kirsten Grabowski, Ivan Yushenko and

Stacey Kyle. If there is anything, anything at all, I can do, please let me know."

Homes paused for a moment of insincere respect before resuming the interview.

"So Mr Jackson, Max, why not spare us the suspense and admit I'm right," Homes was grinning like a shark moving in for the kill, "You are the Real Rock Restaurant Ripper."

Jackson laughed loudly, his expensive veneers gleaming, "Sorry Mr Holmes, I'm afraid I'm not. And the Metropolitan Police have already checked my alibis, so you're going to have to look elsewhere for a viable suspect."

"But have they *really* checked your alibis, Max?" Homes pushed, "My sources suggest that detectives haven't even spoken to your shrink yet. The one you said you were meeting on Tuesday night when Paolo was butchered."

"Obviously you realise I have no control over the Met Police, nor how they conduct their investigations," Jackson gave his own superficial smile, "However, it would be nice if they could clear me to your satisfaction."

Now it was Homes' turn to laugh loudly, "That would take some doing Max. But you're more than welcome to try and convince me."

Jackson shrugged, "I can assure you, I have nothing, *nothing*, to do with the murders. I have witnesses, phone location data and CCTV footage to prove my whereabouts when each of the killings took place. I'm afraid you're going to have to find yourself another suspect."

"In the age of artificial intelligence, government surveillance, deepfakes and computer trickery, I will always, *always* be somewhat sceptical. But I would certainly be interested in seeing your evidence for myself, Max," Homes sounded uncertain for the first time, "Perhaps I could even do some of the Met's legwork for them."

He arched an eyebrow knowingly at the camera.

"Of course, no problem at all. I would be happy to."

"I look forward to that. So on to other matters," Homes segued away, "Why not tell our viewers about the memorials you have set up to honour your employees."

"Colleagues, I prefer to call them colleagues because they were my *family*," Jackson smarmed.

"Fine, tell us about the memorials you have created for each of your *colleagues*," Homes rolled his eyes theatrically as he stressed the word 'colleagues'.

"Yes so, we wanted to create a personalised commemoration for Paolo, Kirsten Ivan and Stacy. First we planned to frame a personal item for each of them, like all the other cool memorabilia we have in all of our restaurants.

"But when we spoke to family and friends, they wanted something more *visceral*. Something that would convey the true horror of what their loved ones had gone through in their final moments. And so with the help of the talented Real Rock Restaurants art team, we have built a full replica of each crime scene in our Greenwich, Camden and Soho restaurants."

The in-studio video cut to pre-recorded footage from the Camden store, showing a very realistic Kirsten waxwork choked and lifeless on the floor. Every detail was present, right down to the sparkly Michael Jackson glove stuffed into her mouth.

"Now I've had the privilege of seeing these new memorials and I have to say they are chilling," Homes was saying, "Realistic, shocking and yet I notice they are also incredibly popular with your customers."

"Yes, they certainly are," Jackson was nodding solemnly, "Incredibly popular."

"So how did you achieve this level of realism?"

"My design team carefully analysed the CCTV footage from each restaurant, faithfully recreating each scene by analysing the video frame-by-frame. Their attention to detail is a true reflection of the respect our family has for each other."

"Well, whether you're the murderer or not, I salute your efforts. And for any *Homes on Homicide* viewers who happen to be in London, or planning a visit, I definitely recommend you drop in and take a look at the tableaus for yourself."

"We welcome anyone, *everyone,* to come down and pay their respects to our fallen colleagues. And if you mention the *Homes on Homicide* show, you can claim a 10% discount on your food order."

A banner flicked up at the bottom of the screen, restating the 10% discount offer and advising parents that the graphic nature of the display may be unsuitable for children.

"Well thank you for coming on my show," Homes proffered his hand for Jackson to shake, "You're still my prime suspect, but I look forward to confirming your alibis for myself."

Misadvertised

"I look forward to it even more," Jackson chuckled.

"That's all we have time for tonight. Thanks again to my guest, Max Jackson, CEO of Real Rock Restaurants. And to Real Rock Restaurants for sponsoring this episode of the *Homes on Homicide* show. Good night!"

Chapter Fifty-One

The darkness was thick, oppressive, total. It wrapped itself around Witz's head like a scratchy black towel, leaving him deaf and blind, his skin crawling and prickling. Arms outstretched, he was stumbling around a large, empty space but there was no light or sound to guide him, no clue as to where he was. But by the smell alone, Witz knew deep in the core of his being that he was was back in the Catacombs. But this time he was in a different part of the tunnels, standing on the edge of infinity and the only way was down.

One foot in front of the other, he edged forward. Or back. Maybe it was up. The total darkness made direction irrelevant, especially as he had nowhere to go, except around in circles. The further he went, the more fearful he became, a feeling like icy water settling in his guts.

The sensation worsened as he became aware of a presence, something next to his left shoulder. "Welcome to my reality Charlie," a voice whispered in his ear. Witz nearly pissed himself in terror, spun round to stare uselessly into the pitch black. There was nothing but more darkness behind him.

"It's a bit shit down here, isn't it?" The voice laughed ironically, "Unsurprising really."

Misadvertised

Wake up, wake up, wake up, Witz screamed at himself, but the darkness swallowed his voice.

"It's lonely down here Charlie," the whisper continued, "I'm all alone except for the Golem - and he's not very talkative. So it's just you and me, Charlie. Will you stay and keep me company?"

No, no, no!

"You know I'm going to keep coming back until I get peace, right?"

Witz couldn't tell if Barry making a promise or a threat. He started running, blundering his way through the black, stumbling and tripping, but never making any progress. And he couldn't get away, the voice was still there, whispering poisonous hate into his ear.

"I'll always be with you, Charlie, *always!*"

Suddenly he was falling, the endless darkness getting deeper. He screamed soundlessly while Barry laughed mercilessly, a harsh, grating sound that made his skin crawl.

The sound was still ringing in his ears when Witz jumped awake, shaking and sweaty, tangled in his bedsheets. Witz tried to free himself, rolling over and coming face to face with Barry, head tilted back at an impossible angle, a look of stupid shock and surprised etched on his lifeless features.

Witz was still screaming when his alarm went off.

Chapter Fifty-Two

"You were right Eva, it's not looking good for this weekend," Carson barked at his speakerphone as he inched his way through the Central London traffic, "How about next weekend?"

"I'm always right, James."

Click. Bzzzzzz. Growl.

"Like you didn't see that coming," Hewson said.

"Hey Siri, play Anberlin," Carson yelled at the car's entertainment system. Immediately the air was filled with thrashing guitars and crashing drums. *Godspeed.*

"Why do you listen to rock music at full volume Guv?" Hewson yelled.

Carson dialled the volume down, "Why would you *not* listen to rock music at full volume? Or are you annoyed by my choice of genre? Do you think that because I'm a detective I should listen to jazz? Or maybe something choral? Opera?

"You watch too much TV, Hewson. No one actually likes jazz. It's just a long-running in-joke between jazz musicians - 'What's the crappiest, most dissonant tune we can play and get away with?' They are just laughing at the beard-stroking idiots who are afraid of looking 'uncool' by admitting that jazz is utter crap."

Hewson wasn't sure she had ever heard her boss this animated before. Apparently she had touched a nerve.

"Think about it. Three or four musicians each doing their own thing at half speed until one of them gets bored. Then they give each other a self-satisfied nod, a sly grin and wait for the beardy chin-strokers to clap. Utterly pretentious toss, a total waste of their musical talent."

Carson paused for a moment and looked hard at his DS, "You don't like jazz do you Hewson?"

"Nope," she shook her head violently, "My musical tastes cross many genres - but they never stray near jazz."

"Glad to hear it," Carson growled, "And to answer your question, rock music is supposed to be played loud."

He turned the music up even louder than before.

Misadvertised

Chapter Fifty-Three

Chief Superintendent Chapman wandered into the murder squad office, "I saw the latest episode of *Homes on Homicide* Hewson, how are you feeling?"

Has everyone seen her choking her guts up? "Not bad considering Guv. Sorry for the embarrassment.'

"Don't apologise Detective Sergeant. If that Homes character had seen what you did, I'm sure he would have had the same reaction. Most normal people would," the Chief Super patted her gently on the shoulder, then moved further into the room.

"I don't mean to intrude," Chapman announced, "But with four dead and an apparent serial maniac on the loose, the senior senior brass are becoming a little agitated."

Carson imagined they were probably phoning Chapman every ten minutes, screaming at him for immediate results. He admired the man's talent for understatement.

"OK sir, here's what we have so far. Four victims, none with any connection to the others except Miklos and Stacey who worked in the same restaurant and who, according to workplace gossip, were in a relationship." He pointed at the photos on the murder wall as he spoke.

"An initial line of enquiry focusing on Nunez's sideline in dealing hash turned out to be a dead-end. Since

Misadvertised

then we have learned that the killer rides a motorbike - DC Oaks is still trawling CCTV footage to trace movements and a registration plate.

"We have also identified a potential motive that suggests the perp is even more unhinged than we thought," Carson scrawled the words *Motive: MUSIC?* on the right hand side of the board, then underlined it several times for emphasis.

"Music?" Chapman raised his bushy silver eyebrows.

"Yes music," Carson explained, "We think the killer is upset by what he sees as 'false advertising'. Not enough actual rock music at the Real Rock Restaurant apparently."

"No bloody way am I taking that to the ACC. Work the angle by all means, but we'll keep it between us for now. Anyway, what kind of a person gets that upset by music?"

"I'm not entirely sure," said Carson, "but it's as good as any other theory right now. Perhaps I'll run it by Doctor Jenkins when we visit him to confirm Max Jackson's alibi this afternoon."

"Yes, you really had better visit the good doctor," Chapman nodded, "I'm getting grief from the brass as to why you have yet to interview Jackson's alibi."

"Aside from the fact he didn't do it," Carson raised an eyebrow, "How does 'the brass' even know whether I have interviewed Doctor Jenkins or not?"

"You haven't heard?" Chapman seemed surprised, "That vlogger guy said so last night in his latest Homes on Homicide update."

"Tell me you don't watch his conspiracy theory nonsense too?"

"Of course I do," Chapman seemed surprised that Carson was surprised, "How else would I know what it happening among the rank and file? Homes seems to know more about what we are doing than I do. In fact *all* of the senior officers I know watch Homes on Homicide - and many are also convinced of Jackson's guilt. They'll probably put money on it when Homes opens his betting channel again."

"Wait, Homes runs a book on active murder cases? Is that even legal?" Carson was shocked but he decided not to dive down that particular rabbit hole, choosing instead to bring the conversation back on topic, "Clearly Max Jackson is a greedy sociopath, but he's not the killer."

"Well it's your investigation, I'll leave you to it. I better get back before my secretary resigns. She really hates taking calls from the Mayor - even when he's in a good mood. Come to think of it, so do I. Ho hum," Chapman paused for a moment then placed a comforting hand on Frank's shoulder, "One suggestion for your own safety - keep your face away from the cameras if you can. There's still a price on your head and people willing and eager to collect.."

Chapman had just walked out when he poked his head back round the door, "Witz. The guy you were in the sewers yesterday, Barry Green, didn't make it home last night. You don't know anything about that?"

Witz paled, "No idea Guv, sorry."

"I just thought I'd ask. His wife's a friend of mine," Chapman shrugged apologetically, "It won't be the first time that Barry's wrapped himself around a bottle somewhere. He's even been known to booze it up down in the tunnels sometimes. I guess he'll head home when the bottle is empty and he sobers up."

"Yeah probably," Witz nodded, head down staring at his desk, willing Chapman to go away and stop asking uncomfortable questions.

Chapman left the office and Carson collapsed back into a nearby swivel chair that promptly tried to unseat him as it span away across the floor. He felt breathless and exhausted, every movement causing him to break out in a sweat, hands shaking like leaves in a stiff breeze.

"Are you OK Guv?" Hewson asked concerned, "You're not looking so hot."

"I assure you Hewson, I am *feeling* very hot right now. Give me a few minutes to get my breath back and we'll go see Doctor Jenkins, try and convince him to circumvent practitioner-patient privilege a little."

Hewson turned her attention back to the team, "Oaks, there's one other thing I need you to do."

The young DC raised an eyebrow questioningly.

"Get someone from uniform to visit a Mr David Reid of 21 Darville Road, Hackney. Tell them to tell him he's too quiet and polite and he needs to stop it immediately. His neighbour thinks he's a serial killer."

"It's always the quiet ones, right?" Woody laughed.

Misadvertised

Chapter Fifty-Four

Carson had Hewson sat in his car outside a smart, four-storey townhouse on the leafy end of Hampstead High Street. The ground floor housed a high-end clothing boutique, while Dr Jenkins operated from a clinic that occupied the upper floors.

The 2pm news headlines finished and Carson sprang out of the car. Hewson jogged to catch him up as he pressed the buzzer on the unobtrusive black door to the left of the boutique. A well-polished brass plaque informed them they had arrived at 'The Laburnum Clinic'.

"Yes?" A woman's voice crackled from the intercom speaker.

"DI Carson and DS Hewson to see Dr Jenkins."

"Do you have an appointment?"

"No madam, we do not. Nor do we need one. We're with the police. Now if you would be kind enough to let us in..."

There was an audible harrumph from the intercom as the door buzzed and the electric lock released. Carson growled and then began climbing the stairs to the first floor, panting heavily with the exertion. He stopped half way up to cough heavily and massage his chest. Hewson followed few steps behind concerned that her boss may be about to have a heart attack.

Misadvertised

As they rounded the landing they were greeted by the harrumpher, a surprisingly short woman clad in brown. Brown skirt, jacket and blouse, brown shoes, tights, hair scraped back and secured in a bun to reveal that even her leather-like skin had been tanned to a matching deep brown shade. Hewson wasn't sure which was more surprising, the fact that it was still possible to buy brown tights or that the woman introduced herself as Ms White. She coughed to disguise her snigger.

"Thank you Ms White," said Carson, oblivious as usual, "Now where can we find Dr Jenkins?"

"He's currently with a client so you'll have to wait," the short brown lady said sniffily, pointing to a frosted glass door to the left of her reception desk, "Please take a seat in the waiting room through there." She pointed at another door to the right.

Carson and Hewson filed into the room as indicated and took a seat in one of the surprisingly plush armchairs on either side of a glass coffee table piled high with magazines.

"I am quite convinced that medical waiting rooms are the only thing keeping the magazine publishing industry in business," said Hewson, reaching for the May 2008 edition of *Chimney Stack Quarterly*, "I mean, who actually buys these titles?"

"Me," replied Carson without a trace of irony, "And that's a great edition. I particularly enjoyed the article on the merits of H-style caps versus full chimney cowls. Starts around page 18 if I remember correctly."

Hewson stared at him for a moment while he searched the pile himself, selecting a well-thumbed copy of *Classic*

Rock. Clearly the conversation was over. She turned to page 18 and began reading about H-style caps. She was so engrossed that she completely missed the arrival of Dr Jenkins, a short, rotund man with an upside-down head. His head was completely bald but a wild, bushy, bright red beard had colonised the lower half of his face. Unnoticed, the doctor was watching both detectives with amusement.

Eventually, Jenkins cleared his throat for the second time and Hewson nearly jumped out of her skin. "I believe you wanted to speak to me?" he said.

"Yes, Dr Jenkins I presume?" Carson tossed his magazine back onto the pile. It teetered for a moment before the entire stack skipped across the table like a stack of dominos. Embarrassed, he stood to shake the doctor's hand while Hewson rushed to tidy up, "I'm DI Carson and this is DS Hewson. We'd just like a few minutes of your time to speak about one of your patients, Max Jackson."

"No problem at all, but we'd best chat in my office. The walls have ears if you know what I mean," the therapist looked pointedly in the direction of Ms White's brown wooden desk.

Once the office door was closed and everyone was seated around another glass-topped coffee table (sans magazines), Jenkins asked, "So how can I be of assistance?"

Carson leaned forward, flipped open his notebook and began to scribble, "As I said, we're here about your patient Max Jackson. We're checking his alibi for the night of the 21st. He says he was here with you between 11pm and 12:30am."

The doctor thought for a moment, then nodded, "Yes, that's right."

"That's a rather late session," Hewson said. She wasn't convinced.

Jenkins continued to nod, "Yes, indeed it is. The Laburnum Clinic operates relatively long and unsociable hours anyway, but Max is one of my penance clients."

"Penance?" Carson raised an eyebrow.

"He's not the only one doing court-mandated therapy for drink driving. I was prosecuted 18 months ago for the same offence. In addition to demanding a hefty fine, the judge saw an opportunity to get something for nothing for the probation service. So now I am working my way through a 500 hour community service order by providing free counselling and therapy to other offenders like Max."

"Better than jail though," Hewson mumbled.

"Yes, absolutely," Jenkins nodded, "Don't get me wrong, I'm not complaining. It just means that I have to complete my penance sessions *after* work. And in Max's case, that sometimes means being here in the middle of the night because of his own inconvenient work schedule. That's the vagaries of the restaurant trade I guess."

Carson sat back in his chair, "Can I run something by you doctor?"

"Certainly. Fire away."

"What sort of person would commit a brutal murder based on something as seemingly ephemeral as music?"

"You think that's the Ripper's motive? Music?" Jenkins brightened up.

"At the moment we're still considering everything," Carson admitted, "Do you think it's a plausible motive?"

"There have been plenty of instances where neighbours are murdered for playing excessively loud music," Jenkins said, "Virtually anyone who is tired, stressed and depressed could be pushed to those kinds of extremes."

"No sorry, I don't think I properly explained myself," Carson shook his head, "I mean someone who commits murder because the *wrong type* of music is being played."

"I'm afraid I don't follow," Jenkins shook his head, "Can you give me an example."

Hewson's scepticism about Carson' theory was growing stronger by the moment. She was enjoying watching him struggle to formulate a scenario without giving away any specific details about the RRR case.

"Imagine you visit a shop called 'The Baroque Boutique' but instead of Bach they are playing blink-182 on the in-store sound system. Most of us would think it odd, but we'd just get on with our day and maybe laugh about it with our friends later on. But are there people who would react in a more extreme, perhaps even violent, way?"

The doctor scratched at his bright orange beard for a moment before answering slowly, "There are some cases where individuals may take that kind of incongruity as a personal slight. Others could treat it as a moral wrong that must be righted, perhaps with violence. Especially if they think that their peaceful requests have been ignored. Because these types of people will certainly have tried a more polite, acceptable approach first, such as writing a letter."

"So these kinds of people do exist. But they must also be incredibly rare, yes?"

"Probably not as rare as you are hoping, detective," Jenkins replied, "I work with many obsessive compulsive patients who could potentially tip over into homicidal rage given the right trigger. And so does every other psychotherapist I know. It's our job to help these people keep themselves regulated so they can align with the expectations and norms of society. But in reality, *everyone*, including you and me, has the potential to commit murder - we're just lucky enough not to have encountered the right combination of triggers. Yet."

"Bloody hell," Hewson muttered under her breath.

"Are there any common traits or behaviours we should be aware of?" Carson continued.

"There may be a few," Jenkins trailed off for a moment, stroking his beard once more, "I would expect the person to demonstrate an obsessive attention to detail. They can see patterns and trends that the rest of us would probably ignore. If they can hold down a job it will be doing something that requires extreme focus, usually working alone. Almost certainly neurodivergent. Probably has some compulsive behaviours too, a repetitive pattern or rhythm or ritual. That could describe half my patients to be honest."

"So we're looking for a twitchy, anti-social accountant?"

"Or detective," Hewson muttered under her breath.

"More likely an actuary or a quant." Jenkins grinned knowingly at her.

"A quant?"

Misadvertised

"A quantitative analyst," Jenkins nodded, "The geniuses who apply mathematics and statistical analysis to the problem of profitable stock market investment and risk management."

"Sounds like a complete banker," said Carson, rising from his chair, "Thanks very much for your time doctor."

As they walked out, Hewson noticed a well-dressed young man sat statue still in the waiting room, hands folded carefully in his lap. He smiled shyly as their eyes met, and Hewson returned it.

"Ah, Julian! Back so soon?" Dr Jenkins greeted his patient, "It's been what, five days? Is everything ok? Come on through to my office."

Carson and Hewson made their way back past the harrumphing Ms Brown, down to the street below.

Chapter Fifty-Five

"Have you got a second Guv?" Witz asked, poking his head around Chapman's door. He hated coming up here to the corridors of power where senior officers tended to lord it over their underlings. Thank God Chapman wasn't like the rest of the senior officers with their university degrees and sod-all policing experience. Even if his office did have the nice, deep pile carpet that was denied to the lower ranks.

"My door's always open DS Witz, you know that," the Chief Super smiled, "Come in, what can I do for you?"

Witz stepped into the room, closed the door and took a seat opposite Chapman, "Well, it's a bit of a delicate matter sir."

"You're not getting married again are you Charlie? Who's the lucky lady?"

Charlie laughed mirthlessly, "No sir. I think my marrying days are now far behind me."

"Is everything ok?" Chapman asked with genuine concern.

If only you knew how not OK I am, Witz thought. Instead he said, "It's about DI Carson. I, we, *the team* are worried about him sir."

"And why are you worried about him?" Chapman's mouth became a straight, thin line.

Well this wasn't going as planned, "We, er, we are worried he's a bit erratic. Jumpy, irritable, unpredictable."

"OK... and?"

"Er, well sir," Witz was sweating now, "We, er. Erm. It's not just natural enthusiasm. We are concerned that he may have a, erm, substance issue."

Chapman stared hard at Witz for a moment. The DS could feel beads of sweat prickling across his forehead.

"I know you're all very competent detectives, so I assume you have already checked Carson' file and that you've spotted the two year gap in his service record?"

For the second day in a row, Witz's shirt was stuck to his back, sweat running down his spine, panic coursing through his veins, "Erm, yes."

Chapman was an increasingly rare example of a senior officer who had done the job, lived the life and knew how other coppers think, "And I suspect that one of the explanations your team has considered is medical leave?"

"Yes," Witz drew the word out slowly, hesitantly.

"Obviously I can't tell you the specifics Charlie, but I can tell you that DI Carson was *not* in rehab or undergoing any kind of addiction treatment. He was on the job the whole time."

Witz nodded dumbly, "Undercover?"

"Like I said Charlie, I can't confirm or deny."

"And he's still adjusting to his old life back in reality. You think that's what is causing his erratic behaviour?"

Chapman nodded, encouraging Witz to continue his train of thought, "*If* he had been undercover for that period of time, I would expect there to be some longer term effects as he adjusts."

"Right…" the DS nodded back, "Although *if* he had been working undercover, he wouldn't be the first officer to return with some very bad habits."

"That's very true. Perhaps I should arrange some random drug tests for your unit," Chapman wasn't nodding encouragingly any more. He wasn't smiling either, "How's your drinking these days Charlie? Do you still have your own tankard behind the bar at The Red Lion."

Witz slumped back into his seat, pale and deeply uncomfortable under Chapman's withering stare.

"Good. I assume we have cleared things up a little," suddenly Chapman was smiling again, "Tell me about your trip into the sewers yesterday. Did Barry chew your ears off about Joseph Balzagette? It's fascinating stuff but he doesn't half go on once he's started."

Witz smiled weakly. *Shit, shit, shit*, "He was very helpful and hospitable sir."

"Did he tell you anything about what he was going to do after you finished down there? Any idea where he may have gone?"

Should he make something up? Point the Guv in the wrong direction? No, keep it simple, "Sorry Guv, nothing at all. Just said he was very busy and he had to go back to work."

Chapman sighed, "Like I said earlier, he'll turn up eventually."

I bloody hope not, thought Witz. He almost ran out of Chapman's office.

Chapter Fifty-Six

"Good afternoon, Metropolitan Police Incident Room. You are speaking to PC Jayawardene. I am recording this call, but everything you tell me will be held in strictest confidence and you can remain anonymous if you prefer. So, what information would you like to share with the detectives?"

"Ah yes, hello, this is Carlos Contreras. You may have seen my show at the Hackney Empire last year?"

"No, Mr Contreras, I'm afraid I haven't seen your show, sorry."

"That's a shame," the disappointment was plain, "The critics said it was one of my best ever shows."

"I'm sure it was sir, but perhaps you could tell me what you know about the murders we are investigating?"

Mr Contreras pulled himself together, "Yes, of course. Now, I was hosting a private séance for Mrs Audley-Farrah, one of my regular clients. She likes to speak to her twin sister who passed over a few years ago…"

"The murders, Mr Contreras?"

"Yes, yes, I was getting to that. Anyway, I was in a deep trance speaking to Jennifer (that's Mrs Audley-Farrah's sister) when we were rudely interrupted by a young man calling himself Paolo."

"Mr Contreras, I hope you are not wasting police time…"

"Certainly not, young lady, I wouldn't dream of it. But this young man, Paolo, was extremely distressed. He had clearly passed over in the most heinous of circumstances. So much so that he could not speak. Well that and the fact he was carrying his own head. But the feeling, the feeling! So young, so sad, so tragic."

Jayawardene's ears pricked up, "He was carrying his head?"

"Yes, tucked under his arm. It would have been quite cartoonish had it not been so gruesome."

That was what was niggling the PC - how did this crank know Paolo had been beheaded? They had definitely held that detail back from the media - and the Nunez family.

"I so desperately wanted to help Paolo, but he could not speak, could not tell me what he wanted. He just made a weird roaring, revving noise. A bit like a motorbike I suppose."

"Just to confirm Mr Contreras, a headless ghost visited you yesterday afternoon and proceeded to make strange motorbike engine noises?" This guy knew too many specific details to be a mere crank, even if the story itself was completely mad.

"Yes, exactly that." Jayawardene could hear the caller nodding like a donkey on speed.

"OK, Mr Contreras, I think the best thing will be to arrange for a detective to come and take a full statement from you in person."

Misadvertised

"Excellent, excellent. They can catch me tonight at the Horse and Groom in Peckham."

They are going to catch you alright mate, Jayawardene thought to herself.

Click.

Misadvertised

Chapter Fifty-Seven

Working on the murder squad, Hewson had had plenty of encounters with death and killers. She knew from personal experience that most murders were committed by perfectly normal people and that most already knew their victims.

However, Jenkins' assertion that everyone has the potential to commit multiple murders was shocking and disturbing - even if she had heard that theory before. What bothered her most was that some people really might decapitate another human being simply for playing the wrong music. She shuddered.

"So Jackson is off the hook then," Carson mumbled, "What else do we have?"

"I guess everything now depends on finding the moped rider," Hewson nodded, "And fast."

Carson had just queued up Pink Floyd's *Wish You Were Here* when the car stereo muted the music to read an incoming SMS from the incident room hotline.

"Weird call from a guy called Carlos Contreras. Seems to know too many confidential details of the Paolo Nunez murder. Recommend further investigation. PC Jayarwarrrrdeenny." Siri murdered the poor officer's surname, "Did you want to reply?"

"No!" Carson yelled, "Call DS Oaks."

She may have been poor at reading named, but Siri did manage to dial Woody's number successfully. On the third attempt.

"Oaks? Good. Go and have a word with PC Jayarwardene over on the incident desk, I think she has an important tip."

"Important? Like the Beast of the Fleet? I doubt it Guv."

"Get it done DC Oaks."

Click.

Misadvertised

Chapter Fifty-Eight

"The Metropolitan Police have this afternoon released more details about the search for the killer known as the Real Rock Restaurant Ripper who is suspected of the murder of four employees. Paolo Nunez, 30, Kirsten Grabowski, 26, Ivan Yushenko, 32, and Stacey Kyle, 27, were brutally murdered in three separate incidents that eyewitnesses describe as 'shocking' and 'horrific'.

Speaking earlier today, Chief Superintendent William Chapman has said they are urgently trying to trace several delivery drivers who may have had a customer collection on the nights in question.

'We would like to speak to anyone who was in the Greenwich restaurant on Tuesday night, the Camden outlet on Wednesday night or the Soho branch on Friday morning.

If you have any information, no matter how seemingly unimportant, please call the incident room on 0207...'"

Misadvertised

Chapter Fifty-Nine

Woody was sceptical but eventually he had agreed to go and see the mysterious Mr Contreras in Peckham. The car park at the Horse and Groom was full so he had reluctantly left his car outside the sketchy looking estate across the road. He fully expected to find it gone, or on fire, when he had finished interviewing the suspicious sounding psychic.

The detective pushed open the saloon bar door and was greeted by a cloud of blue cigarette smoke. He looked at the tar-stained ceiling and the holes burned into the threadbare brown-and-red carpet., Clearly patrons of the Horse and Groom had never abided by the seventeen year-old national smoking ban. He shouldered his way through the saloon bar and out through the rear door to the dimly lit function room that looked not unlike a barn. Or an old bus depot.

A makeshift stage stood against the far wall and a rounded, middle-aged man with a comedy moustache stood in the smoky spotlight. He clutched a microphone in one hand and used the other to massage his temples as he addressed his audience, just like every other psychic Woody had ever seen on TV.

A few rows of fold-up metal chairs had been placed in front of the stage, occupied mostly by fractionally interested elderly men and women, chain-smoking foul-smelling contraband cigarettes, no doubt purchased at a pension-friendly price from an entrepreneurial wide boy on the housing estate opposite. Elsewhere a crowd of young boys were fooling around in the corner, drunk, heckling the psychic onstage.

Woody decided to remain at the back of the room where he could see everyone. He leaned against the wall, crossed his arms and settled in to watch what was left of the show.

Contreras was trying his best, communing with the spirits of the recently departed, even taking a few minutes to speak to one old lady's cat.

"I have the name 'Tiddles'. Has someone here recently lost a furry friend named Tiddles?"

An elderly woman tentatively raised her hand and a murmur of sympathy rippled through the audience.

"Ah good Mrs...?" Contreras prompted her.

"Mrs Anderssen."

"Tiddles says he is very..."

"She," Mrs Anderssen interrupted.

"Sorry the connection is not strong, *she* is very faint. I can just hear her though. She wants you to know that she is safe and well-fed and that she has found a lovely warm spot to sleep," he paused for a moment, brow furrowed as though he was straining to hear a voice from far away. Mrs Anderssen leaned forward in anticipation.

"She also says that she's looking forward to seeing you very soon," Contreras finished.

"But...she's dead?" Mrs Anderssen's voice began to quaver, a mix of grief and terror.

Misadvertised

"Yes, I know," replied Contreras before realising what Tibbles had just said.

Apparently although Mrs Anderssen missed her cat a lot, she wasn't so thrilled by the suggestion she would shortly be 'crossing over' to join her dearly departed feline friend. She burst into tears. The audience murmurs of sympathy were becoming muttered curses and threats aimed at the psychic.

At that point Contreras knew he had lost the crowd and brought the show to a quick conclusion, announcing loudly over Mrs Thursgood's escalating sobs, "That's all for tonight. You've been a wonderful audience, thank you. Private readings are available after the show in my dressing room." No one attempted to follow him out, although the rowdy crew whistled and cheered ironically as he shuffled out of the room.

Woody peeled away from the wall, surprised he hadn't left the sleeve of his jacket stuck to the layer of grime that covered everything, and sauntered out the back of the function room. Contreras' dressing room was little more than a cupboard with two hard wooden chairs and a grimy mirror propped on a desk below a bare lightbulb.

"Ah, come in, come in!" The psychic seemed genuinely shocked that anyone wanted a private reading. Immediately his eyes narrowed as he tried to size up Woody - and the depth of his pockets.

Woody shuffled in sideways, allowing Contreras to close the door behind him. Then he shuffled back around to the front of the chair. There was so little room to move that when he and Contreras sat, their knees touched. Woody tried to push his chair backwards, but it was already pressed against the wall.

"So what can I do for you young man? Is there someone dearly departed you would like me to contact on your behalf? Need some guidance for your love life? Career perhaps?"

"Er no, no thank you Mr Contreras. I'm actually here on police business. I believe my colleague, PC Jayawardene, said a detective would come to take a statement? Well that's me."

"Oh," the last of the showman's energy and enthusiasm drained away and the man visibly sagged in his chair. Woody almost felt sorry for him, but the touching knees situation was really starting to bother him.

"Yes of course. I thought perhaps she was joking. She didn't seem to take my report very seriously."

"To be honest Mr Contreras, it's not every day we get a call from a psychic with specific, confidential details of the crimes we're investigating." *Just lots and lots of nut jobs*, he thought.

"Well I was visited by Paolo, and then I saw the appeal on TV so I knew I *had* to call."

"Right Mr Contreras, but we have a problem. As I said, some of the information you shared with my colleague was extremely sensitive, never released to the press. Or to anyone else for that matter," there was something hostile in the way the psychic was staring at him, but the DC pressed on, "You knew some *very* specific details about the murder. Things you shouldn't know unless you were there. Do you see our problem?"

Contreras gave him a bemused look, "Of course not. Don't you think the spirit of a murder victim knows the details of their own death?"

"Look, I'm not going to get into the metaphysics of it with you. Where were you on Tuesday night?"

"I was doing a show out in Mitcham. Another faceless, characterless dive like this," he waved his hands vaguely at the cupboard they were sat in, "Obviously you can check it out, give the landlord over at The Old Leather Bottle a call to confirm. And if you're lucky, one of the usual skeptics is bound to have uploaded a clip to TikTok or YouTube or whatever."

OK, let's say you weren't in Greenwich. I'm still not satisfied with your answer and I *will* arrest you if you don't tell me exactly what you know - and how."

The psychic stared at Woody hard, then shrugged and sighed. It didn't seem possible, but Contreras continued to crumple. He was broken, "I saw it on Instagram."

"You did what?"

"Some no-name wannabe influencer posted a blurry photo of the crime scene on their Instagram story in the hope of attracting new followers. Apparently she got there before the police, snapped a pic, uploaded it quickly and sat back waiting for the clicks."

"What was the user name?"

"@Owly_LAss575," Contreras spelled it out carefully so that Woody could write it in his notebook. He then thought better of it, bashing the name into his smartphone so he could check it out now. Sure enough 'Medium Extraordinaire', Olwen of Old Oak Common had a blurred photo of the blood-soaked Greenwich crime scene at the top of her feed. The DC wondered how the Met Police had failed to find the pic until he saw Olwen had just 56 followers - including Contreras.

"And she just happens to be one of your rivals in the fraud and fakery trade I notice."

"Whatever," Contreras shrugged belligerently, "I'm just trying to make a living."

"Yes," nodded Woody, "at the expense of the nearly dead."

#

At the best of times Woody was freaked out by psychics. Even more so when he had to rub knees with them. He climbed back into his car, thankfully all four wheels were still in place. Settled in, doors locked, he sent a quick text message to Carson,

#

> Spoke to Contreras. Full details tomorrow but can confirm, he's NOT our man.

#

As he drove away from Peckham, he made a call to the City of London Police Action Fraud team.

"Hi this is DC Oaks from Marylebone CID. I need to make a take-down request for an Instagram post. Got a pen handy? The user name is @Owly_LAss575…"

Misadvertised

Chapter Sixty

It was fast approaching midnight and Carson was fighting to keep his eyes open. Sleeping in the shed wasn't ideal, but then he didn't think he had slept more than a few hours each night since moving out here, a few months earlier. Some nights he hadn't slept at all. Sheer exhaustion may explain the racing heart and tremors, but why couldn't he sleep? If he was overweight and severely out of shape, it might make sense. But he wasn't completely unfit, didn't carry too much weight and ate relatively healthily thanks to Eva. It had to be plain old stress, he assumed. Not that that made sense given what he had been through in the past two years - even on the worst day, the murder squad was a cakewalk.

He rubbed his eyes, trying to stop them blurring so he could squint at his notebook. It was covered in scrawls and arrows, underlined words and scribbled out sentences. Like the case, it was a complete mess and his shaking hands were making his handwriting almost illegible. Even if he had successfully identified the motive, he had absolutely nothing to work with in regards to suspects.

Male?, average height, physically fit, motorcyclist, forensically-aware, sociopath. Nothing, not a single thread that he could pull at. All he needed was a lead, something to tug on that would unravel this unholy mess and lead him to the killer. He tossed the notebook aside angrily.

Eva hadn't left any food out tonight and his stomach grumbled angrily. He couldn't tell whether this was a pointed punishment or whether she had just forgotten. He didn't really care either, just wanted to know she was ok. He looked out the shed window and studied the darkened house for a few minutes, trying to discern whether Eva was still awake. But the curtains were shut fast and the back door locked, so he would never know for sure.

He sighed, stared angrily at the notebook where it lay on top of his pile of clothes. Finally, he lay back and snuggled down into his sleeping bag. For the first time in weeks he felt like he may actually sleep. Seconds later, he was gone.

Misadvertised

Chapter Sixty-One

"Well, well, well," Sherlock Homes gurned at the camera, "It seems like the Real Rock Ripper case may be gaining some traction. Finally! First, the good news. There were no murders at a Real Rock Restaurant last night. Well done Met Police!"

Somehow Homes was able to make his applause sound sarcastic.

"However, a pause in the killings does raise some important questions…"

Homes held up a gloved hand and began counting on his fingers, "One, is the killer done? He's delivered his message, so have his demands been met? Unless our friend Max Jackson made a large cash payment in used bills, I suspect not."

A big red cross flashed up on screen.

"Second, why no killing last night? Is the killer a practicing believer, refusing to work on the Sabbath? Highly unlikely given what God has to say about murder."

The red cross flashed on screen again.

"Third, is he lying low because the Police are getting closer? Is his neck getting itchy as the rozzers prepare to feel his collar?" Homes paused as if to consider the point himself, "This one could be possible. Our intrepid team of Met detectives were spotted in Hampstead earlier today,

Misadvertised

going to visit a certain Doctor Jenkins. Now those of you who have been following my social media updates on the Ripper case closely will remember that my prime suspect," a picture of Max Jackson flashed up on screen, "claimed that he was visiting his therapist, a certain Doctor Jenkins, at the time of Paolo Nunez's murder. You know, some time approaching midnight on Tuesday."

Homes paused and stroked his chin sarcastically, "Mmmm...Jimmy Hill."

"However, the police seem to have been satisfied by Doctor Jenkins' version of events because they have not yet made any arrests. So it's possible that as Max Jackson feels the net tightening around him, he's been scared into hiding. Or maybe he's just taking his time, freely wandering the streets of London, preparing a gruesome ending for his next victim."

Homes shrugged theatrically for the camera, "I know which one my money is on..."

"And speaking of money, I would just like to let you, my loyal subscribers, know that the Real Rock Ripper Gaming Room, sponsored by Real Rock Restaurants, is now open. You can join the hunt for the killer *and* enjoy the opportunity to win some cash too."

The screen filled with text, a whole range of betting options related to the case. There were odds available for time to arrest, scene of the next murder, total body count and many more.

"Unfortunately, the odds on Max Jackson being charged with murder are low, currently 1 to 3, but there's still money to be made if you want to take a chance. Why not build your own accumulator? Log on, take a look, and

Misadvertised

join the chase today! Over 18s only. Please gamble responsibly."

Misadvertised

Chapter Sixty-Two

Woody was sat in the circle of blinding white cast by a giant spotlight. He couldn't see them, but somewhere in the darkness off to his right, a large audience was staring at him, waiting for the entertainment to begin. He squirmed uncomfortably on the hard wooden chair, the heat generated by the powerful spotlight making his brow prickle with sweat.

"So, Mr Oaks," an instantly recognisable theatrical voice said to him from the other side of the stage, somewhere just outside the circle of light, "I have a message for you from the other side."

"Actually Contreras, before you go any further, it's *Detective Constable* Oaks."

"Of course it is, of course it is," Contreras said, his voice tinged with irritation, "Well, *Detective Constable* Oaks, I have a message from your dearly departed grandmother."

"Hold on," Woody interrupted again, "My gran isn't dead."

"No, the other one," Contreras tried again.

"Grandma Kath isn't dead either."

"Are you sure?" Contreras stepped into the circle of light, leaned forward towards Woody, raising a questioning eyebrow.

Misadvertised

"Yes," Woody nodded, "I'm very sure."

"Bugger," the medium muttered, raising an appreciative titter from the shadowed audience, "Wait, he's saying something else... Barry. Barry, not Granny."

"I don't know a Barry either."

There was another ripple of laughter from the audience, louder this time. Woody squinted against the light, trying to see who was out there. The crowd sounded much larger than the one at The Horse and Groom. He wondered if Mrs Thursgood or her cat were watching, laughing.

"Listen son," Contreras was getting angry, "Whoever Barry is, he's very upset and he wants me to communicate a message *to you*. Yes you, Detective Constable Oaks. He says, 'Don't leave me down here with the Golem'."

Something flickered vaguely in Woody's subconscious subconscious, "I think you've got the wrong dude, Carlos, you need to speak to Witz. He was the one who was told to investigate the Golem lead."

There was another ripple of laughter from the audience. Contreras shot Woody a murderous look, then turned to give his patrons an enormous, forced smile, his arms held wide, "Ladies and gentlemen, the one and only DC Oaks!"

There was a thunder of applause as Contreras helped Woody to his feet, even joining in the clapping as the policeman took an embarrassed bow. It went on and on, encore after encore, until he grew to enjoy the moment, the raw adulation of the crowd. *His* crowd, chanting his name.

Woody! Woody! Woody!

Misadvertised

The sound of clapping and foot stamping was still ringing in his ears when his alarm went off, waking him for his pre-shift shower.

Chapter Sixty-Three

"Guv, I've got something!" Woody yelled, thumping a fist on his desk.

Carson dropped the egg mayonnaise sandwich that Eva had made him for lunch, sprinted from his office and thundered over to Oaks' desk, "What? What have you got?"

"I've been cross-referencing the info we got from the FeedMeNow app and I found a link. There's one driver who was at all three restaurants on the nights in question."

"Bloody hell," said Hewson, slapping him on the back, "Nice one Woody."

"Nice one indeed, DC Oaks," Carson nodded impressed, "Now who is this driver, and where can we find them?"

"Mr Charles Kingston of Polygon Road, out the back end of St Pancras. No criminal record though."

"Nothing? Not even any juvenile arrests or cautions?" Carson was scribbling every detail down in his notebook.

"Nope, the guy is completely clean. He's never even received a parking ticket, let alone a conviction."

Carson drummed his knuckles on the desk, thinking. "It's quite a step up from Boy Scout to serial murderer," he said after a moment, "But we had better bring Mr Kingston in for a chat, sharpish. Get the team together and I'll let the Chief Super know."

Misadvertised

Chapter Sixty-Four

Chapman had insisted his team take no chances, so Carson had been forced to call in MO19. Which meant that he had had to stand aside so the Met's firearms officers could make the actual arrest of *his* suspect. Carson' team had been allowed to sit in on the operational briefing, but MO19 Sergeant Turner made it clear that they would not be playing any active role in the arrest. He did this by telling them to sit down, shut up and stay shut up for the duration. Meanwhile the tactical team were busy tightening the velcro straps on their body armour, polishing their protective visors and checking ammunition clips.

"Our target is a suspect in four exceptionally violent murders, and the Ops Commander has warned that the use of deadly force may be necessary. You," he pointed at Carson, "are to stay outside the operational theatre until I tell you it is safe to do so. Do you understand?"

Carson nodded then muttered under his breath, "Bastards."

"What?"

"Yes, of course, Sergeant Turner."

The Ops Commander stared hard at Carson for a few moments, willing him to either repeat the slur or back out of the operation entirely. Carson countered with a wide, innocent grin of his own. Eventually the armed copper span on his combat booted heel and stomped away.

The tactical support team swept out of the briefing room behind him, a surge of black armour and deadly steel, making their way out to two waiting Trojan armed response vehicles. As soon as they were loaded, the Trojans sped up the ramp leading out of the carpark below the police station. Carson and Hewson chased after them in the black Audi, trying to keep up with their armed colleagues. Carson suspected Sergeant Turner may try and lose them on the way out of spite. Evans, Witz and Oaks trailing behind in another car - the senior detective wasn't much of a pursuit driver.

As Carson fought to keep up with the tactical support team vehicles, Hewson followed a red dot on her smartphone screen that was weaving through the backstreets of Marylebone. The dot slowed as the rider arrived in one of the many park-centred squares that dot London.

"He's slowing down," she muttered.

"As are our gung-ho colleagues," said Carson stamping on the brakes to avoid hitting the Trojan which had stopped sharply, now blocking the road in front. The armed officers had begun piling out before the ARV had even stopped.

Behind it Hewson could see where a moped had pulled up on the pavement outside one of the many terraced townhouses common to this area. The building had been converted into ultra-trendy, over-priced, half empty offices. The sort of places that hip young IT startups and fashionable venture capital unicorns choose to fill with sleep pods, pool tables, yoga mats, vegan coffee bars and for the unfortunate schmuck who had to do some actual work, an occasional desk.

The rider hopped nimbly off his bike and began rummaging in the parcel box mounted on the back behind the pillion. He was completely oblivious to the black-clad armed police who had surrounded him, every gun levelled for a potential kill shot. Carson and Evans leaped out of their car, standing behind the ARV just in case someone started shooting.

"Charlie Kingston, this is the police. Stand still and raise your hands above your head, NOW!" Sergeant Turner roared.

Unable to hear the instruction, the moped rider continued to shuffle items around in the bag. It was impossible to see what they were actually reaching for, ratcheting up the tension and uncertainty. Hewson could see the firearms officers readying for action, worried that the suspect was about to produce a weapon. If there was a weapon, MO19 needed to act immediately, putting the suspect down before they could injure anyone else.

"Charlie Kingston. Place your hands behind your head, interlock your fingers and turn to face me!"

"He can't hear," Carson muttered to Hewson. "He can't hear you through his crash helmet!" He yelled at the MO19 sergeant.

If the firearms officer heard Carson, he made no acknowledgement. "Charlie Kingston, this is your final warning. Place your hands behind your head, interlock your fingers and turn to face me. Now!"

Misadvertised

"They can't hear you, you idiot!" Carson was becoming breathless and agitated as the situation spiralled out of control, face reddening by the second "We don't even know if the suspect is armed and they're about to shoot him." He moved from behind the Trojan and began running towards the suspect.

"Stop him!" the sergeant yelled. One of his masked colleagues grabbed Carson on the way past and the two men grappled, falling to the ground as the DI tried to prevent a tragedy.

The rider finally noticed the commotion and whirled around to see what was happening. There was a loud crack as one of the armed police fired. The delivery rider looked as though they had been hit by an enormous, invisible punch to the torso, stumbling quickly backwards. Then they crumpled backwards onto the pavement, crash helmet bouncing loudly on the flagstones, a plastic bag full of curry and rice falling from their hand. The sound of smashing glass from the window behind the rider added a final audio equivalent of the cherry on top.

"Bollocks," said Hewson as the scene descended into chaos.

Misadvertised

Chapter Sixty-Five

When Chief Superintendent Chapman arrived on the scene, he found three groups of extremely pissed off people. The MO19 tactical support team crowded around one of the Trojans where a distraught officer was being processed after discharging his firearm. Sergeant Turner was whispering instructions to the rest of his team, preparing a coherent story for them to deliver at the inevitable debrief and inquiry to follow. On the other side of the street, Chapman's murder squad detectives stood beside Carson' car, staring daggers at their armed colleagues, annoyed at the shooting of their prime suspect and the mountain of paperwork that the shooting would bring with it.

A pair of uniformed constables worked at both ends of the short terrace, taping off the road and trying to prevent any rubberneckers, including Sherlock Homes, trampling the scene. Faces peeped out from the windows surrounding the square, office workers keen to see what was going on, each enjoying the thrill of knowing that their window could potentially be shot out too. In fact, many brandished smartphones, videoing the scene in the hope of catching something gruesome - blood and violence always goes viral on social media.

Misadvertised

Every minute that passed saw more marked cars and reinforcements pull up outside the cordon. Already half the Metropolitan Police force seemed to be swarming around the small square, most of the officers looking lost, disoriented and surplus to requirements. Still, the show of might would give the Mayor and the upper echelons of the Force something to feel warm and fuzzy about - even if the shooting was hugely embarrassing.

In the middle of the chaos, two paramedics were knelt on the pavement, covered in spilled curry and rice, working on Charlie Kingston. The suspect had been shot high on the left-hand side of the chest, somehow missing everything vital, bullet passing through the shoulder just above the lung. Charlie was clearly in a lot of pain however, his screaming could be heard through the open visor of his motorcycle helmet. Hardly surprising when you consider he had been hit by a red hot 5.56 bullet travelling at more than 2000 miles per hour, drilling a hole right through his body on its way to who knows where inside the building behind.

"It's nasty, but he'll survive," the lead paramedic informed Carson, "You're not looking so good yourself officer, do you want me to check you over?"

"No thanks. Let me know when you're ready to move Kingston," the DI said, coughing and wheezing, "One of my team will have to ride along."

The paramedic nodded and Carson walked jerkily back to his team as Chapman fought his way under the police tape barrier.

"What the hell happened?" The Chief Superintendent demanded of his lead detective.

Misadvertised

"The short version? Because of his helmet, the suspect failed to hear warnings issued by the TST. TST got antsy. TST shot the suspect," he gestured uselessly at the leather-clad figure writhing in pain on the pavement.

"He's telling the truth Chief Superintendent," someone called from the crowd of onlookers, "I saw everything. DI Carson tried to save the motorcyclist."

"Oh bloody hell, it's Homes," Hewson muttered, "How did he get here so quickly?"

"Wanker must have followed us from BPR," Woody said, "Maybe we could do him for a traffic violation? He must have been speeding to keep up with us…"

Hewson looked away, desperate not to be caught on film again.

Chapman turned to face the crowd, "I'm sure a uniformed officer will come and take your statement soon Mr Homes. Now if you don't mind, please piss off. We've got some real detective work to do."

Homes stared at Chapman belligerently, phone held outstretched so that he could record this interaction - and anything else that might happen. His subscribers expected - no demanded - that he capture everything for their vicarious pleasure on this evening's broadcast. The Assistant Constable glared angrily at the amateur sleuth, then turned his bulky body away as rapidly as he could.

The Chief Super sighed, then rubbed his face with his hands, "The Assistant Chief Constable is going to lose his mind. And as for the Mayor…" He trailed off. Carson waited impassively. "Do we even know if this guy *is* the murderer?"

Misadvertised

Hewson shook her head, "No one has had a chance to speak to him yet, let alone arrest him."

"Evans, get over there and read him his rights," Chapman gestured at the man on the pavement, "Then I want you all back at the station to write up your reports. You need to get a head start on the paperwork because we've still got four murders to solve in between all the additional bureaucracy this mess will bring."

As the body responsible for investigating every officer involved shooting incident in the UK, Carson was surprised reps from the Independent Police Complaints Commission were not already here to further complicate matters.

"All clear?"

The team nodded, Oaks and Witz hurrying back to his car. Evans finished cautioning the suspect then jogged to catch up her two colleagues. The paramedics had loaded Kingston onto a stretcher and were preparing to put him in the back of an ambulance. His cries of pain had lessened, clearly the morphine was working.

"That was a total cock-up," Hewson said, watching the paramedics work, "But the shooting was a accident. What will happen to the officer who pulled the trigger?"

"I have no idea," said Carson, "But given the IPCC's track record, he will probably be charged and put on trial - they would rather someone else, like a jury, makes the final decision about culpability."

"Poor bastard," Hewson shot the MO19 officers a look of compassion, "Do you want me to ride in the ambulance and you follow along in your car?"

"Sounds like a plan."

Chapter Sixty-Six

Carson had followed the ambulance for a couple of blocks when his phone rang.

"Guv, I think we've got a problem," it was Hewson calling from the vehicle in front.

"How so?"

"Humour me for a moment. What was the description of Charlie Kingston again?"

"Black male, approximately six feet tall, 190 pounds. Last seen sporting a short beard."

"OK, we definitely have a problem. The paramedics were concerned about Kingston's oxygen levels so they took a risk and removed his helmet."

"And?"

"And Charlie Kingston seems to have turned into an IC4 female, approximately five feet five inches tall and weighing I dunno, 140 pounds?"

"Are you suggesting Kingston somehow transformed into a short woman after being shot?"

"No Guv, I was joking. I don't think this is Charlie Kingston at all."

Misadvertised

Chapter Sixty-Seven

"Breaking news this hour. Metropolitan Police sources confirm a man has been shot by armed response officers conducting an operation in Marylebone this afternoon.

Details remain sketchy but eyewitnesses report the police opened fire after the man failed to respond to repeated demands to surrender. Popular true crime blogger and amateur detective Sherlock Homes witnessed the shooting and spoke to our reporter on the scene:

'There were five or six officers all wearing black, full masks and everything. Big guns too. They were yelling at this delivery guy to get on the floor but he didn't seem to hear them, just kept fiddling in his bag on the back of his bike. Then this other officer, a detective, he was yelling at the armed police, running towards the delivery guy. Next thing I know, there's a loud bang and the delivery guy is on the ground bleeding. Don't think he was dead though.'

We'll update you with more details as soon as we receive them.

In other news, Police are appealing for missing local man Barry Green to get in touch. Green, aged 38, disappeared on Saturday, sometime after 3pm in the Camden area. He is described as being 5'7", 160lbs with short brown hair and was last seen wearing a black t-shirt,

Misadvertised

black rubber waders and an orange hi viz jacket. Anyone who may have information about Barry's whereabouts should contact the Metropolitan Police missing persons hotline on 0207..."

Misadvertised

Chapter Sixty-Eight

By the time the ambulance arrived at St Mary's Hospital in Paddington, "Charlie Kingston"'s condition had been stabilised. Carson had caught his breath and slowed his racing heartbeat, easing the burning pain in his chest. Hewson had managed to convince the triage nurse to place the injured rider in a private room while she waited to be seen by a doctor. Kingston herself looked pale but relaxed, the intravenous morphine administered by the paramedics after the shooting seemed to be having the desired effect. Pain dulled, she seemed to be surprisingly lucid.

As soon as the nurse left, Carson spoke up, "Just to remind you that you are still under caution Charlie. Do you understand?"

The woman nodded weakly as Hewson handcuffed her wrist to the rail running along the side of her hospital bed.

"So, who are you?" Carson demanded impatiently. Hewson gave him a look as if to say, *she's been shot, tread carefully boss*. As usual, Carson missed the subtlety, "Do you speak English? What is your name?"

"Charlie Kingston," the young woman whispered in a heavy accent, "Yes, I speak English. I am Charlie Kingston."

Misadvertised

"No, you're not," Carson barked. Hewson made a hand gesture to suggest that he tried to keep the volume down. "I've checked and you're not Charlie Kingston," he continued a little more quietly.

"I am," the woman nodded a little more emphatically, "I am Charlie Kingston."

"Charlie Kingston is a tall, black man in his early 40s. He's also wanted in connection with four brutal, sadistic murders," the DI paused to give the young woman a chance to digest what he had just said, "Are you *sure* you're Charlie Kingston?"

The woman looked as though she was about to cry. "No," she whispered.

"No," Hewson took over, adopting a more soothing tone, "So shall we try again? What is your name?"

"Razia Qazi," she sighed.

"And why are you pretending to be Charlie Kingston, Razia?"

"Because I am an illegal," this time she did start to cry, "Please don't send me back. Please, please don't send me back. I can't go back to Kandahar."

"I'm not here from immigration services, Razia, I'm not interested in that. But I do need to know where you were on Tuesday night."

"Tuesday night?" Razia was struggling, fear and the dulling effects of the morphine slowing her down, "I was working."

"Delivering food for the FeedMeNow app?"

"Yes."

"And did you make any collections from the Real Rock Restaurant in Greenwich?"

Misadvertised

For a moment, the only sound was Carson scribbling furiously in his notepad.

"Yes…" Razia was hesitant.

"And Wednesday night? Where were you?"

"At home."

"Not working? You weren't in Camden?"

"No, Tuesday and Thursday are my nights. No app work on Wednesday."

"What do you mean 'your nights'?" Carson broke in.

"Other people work Wednesday and Friday and at the weekends."

"Sorry Razia, I don't understand," Hewson took over again.

"There are four of us. We live together, take turns to work on the app."

"So what about Charlie Kingston, which nights does he work?"

"Every night. We are all 'Charlie Kingston'."

"Wait, are you saying Charlie Kingston doesn't exist?" Carson could feel another prime suspect slipping away.

"We are illegals, we cannot get jobs. So we share a fake ID, Charlie Kingston, for the FeedMeNow app. It is the only way we can work to earn money and why I cannot work Wednesday. Are you going to send me back to Afghanistan?"

Hewson shook her head, "I don't know what will happen Razia. We will need to speak to the other delivery drivers, but it looks like you have been the victim of a terrible misunderstanding. I'm so sorry for what happened to you today."

Misadvertised

Carson growled. Back to square one.

Misadvertised

Chapter Sixty-Nine

Back in Marylebone, when the finger pointing and recriminations had finally died down, Chapman had cleared his remaining detectives to return to Balls Pond Road. Witz, Evans and Woody sat in stunned silence for the first few minutes as the junior detective drove them away from the scene. None of them had ever witnessed a suspect being shot before, and Witz had seen most things over the course of his long career.

Eventually Woody broke the silence, "What did Chapman say when you spoke to him about Carson?"

"The Chief Super said we should leave Carson alone."

"That's it?" Evans asked, "He didn't suggest you make a formal complaint or anything?"

"Nope, quite the opposite. He heavily intimated that we should butt out."

Woody whistled through his teeth, "So the Chief Super is covering for the coke head antics of his DI? What does Carson have on Chapman?"

"No Woody, there's no conspiracy here," Witz shook his head, "Chapman implied that the gap in Carson' service record is because he was working deep undercover and that's why he is the way he is."

"Implied?" Evans raised an eyebrow quizzically.

"Well he couldn't come out and just say it, could he?" Witz sighed, "Especially if the operation or any prosecutions resulting from it are still ongoing. He just suggested that two years living a lie in the field does bad things to a person."

"But what if those bad things include developing a full-blown coke habit?" Woody asked.

"When I asked, Chapman threatened to 'randomly' drug test us all."

Silence fell over the car again for a few minutes. Random drug tests were overseen by the professional standards team and no one wanted to tangle with them, ever.

Misadvertised

Chapter Seventy

"Good afternoon, Metropolitan Police Incident Room. You are speaking to PC Jayawardene. Just to make you aware, this call is being recorded but you are free to remain anonymous if you prefer. How can I help you?"

"Hi, I'd like to report an attempted murder." This caller sounded particularly young.

"Are you calling about a new crime? If so, I'll need you to hang up and dial 999 instead," the PC advised.

"Yeah, it's a new crime. I just saw a copper shoot an unarmed civilian in the street. Geezer on a moped, he ain't done nuffin and this bastard pig shoots him down in cold blood. Braaap Braaap! That's murder innit."

"Right. If you're a witness to a shooting, I'll need your contact details so one of our officers can take a statement."

"After seeing a pig shoot an unarmed man in the street? No chance."

Click.

PC Jayawardene hoped the murder squad solved this case soon - she wasn't sure if she could stand another day on the incident room hotline. Even an icy, wet January day spent marshalling drunken Arsenal fans outside the Emirates Stadium would be preferable to this madness.

Misadvertised

Chapter Seventy-One

"Finally we have some good news," Carson was standing by the murder wall, to address his team, "There were no triple-R murders last night. Unfortunately that's all we have. Our prime suspect, Charlie Kingston, does not exist and none of the four people pretending to be him have any crossover with the dates and times in question. So please, someone, tell me you have another angle we can investigate?"

"I've noticed that online interest in RRR is now off the scale. Mainstream media is obsessed with identifying the killer and assigning blame - currently we are top of the hit list. The dark tourism communities are on fire - someone is already offering a pub crawl tour of the restaurants. And London has shot to the top of the dark tourism rankings with nutcases from around the world adding RRR to their bucket lists. Is it worth looking into them?" Witz asked.

"To be fair, most of them are bandwagon-jumpers,' Hewson said, "They love to gawp, revel in the notoriety and being edgy, but I doubt they have the stomach for what we've seen."

"I agree with Hewson, they are probably nothing but a noisy, annoying sideshow that will quickly drain all of our resources if we go too far down that rabbit hole,"

Carson nodded, "Run the names of the noisiest and/or creepiest ones through the PNC. But don't spend too long on it. Fob it off to PC Jayawardene to do in between hotline calls."

He thought for a minute, "What are our collective thoughts about that Homes guy? General nuisance or potential suspect?"

"He's just a nuisance Guv," Evans said, "Homes will make our lives hell with his video blog, he always does. Somehow he has access to far more insider info than he should but he's not a killer. Again, he loves being edgy but I'd bet he probably still lives at home with his mother."

"And I bet that's not one of the odds available on his new gambling website," Woody snarked.

"Bugger," Carson sighed, "But you know Norman Bates lived at home with his mother too, right?"

Witz sniggered but Evans' blank look showed she was far too young to understand the reference.

Woody raised his hand, "I've finished trawling all the footage we collected from North Greenwich and Camden. If Witz or Evans could help we should be able to finish Soho today too."

"Have you found anything workable yet?"

"Lots and lots of motorcycles and mopeds. And not just FeedMeNow app delivery drivers either. London is full of the bastard things."

"It's the only way to get around the Mayor's bastard congestion charge," Carson growled, "Get uniform to help you with the mopeds. We're going to have to trace - and eliminate – every single one."

Misadvertised

Hewson delivered her assessment, "Big sweaty, hairy balls."

Chapter Seventy-Two

"Yes!" Oaks yelled, thumping his desk in excitement, "I found it!"

"Found what Woody?" Witz demanded.

"I found the missing piece, the needle in the haystack, *the moped*!"

"Really?"

"Well I have identified a single registration plate that was seen in the vicinity of all three crime scenes at approximately the right times. Does that count?"

"OK," said Carson, taking control, "Read it out to me."

"HH56 SWM"

Carson transcribed each letter and number onto a yellow sticky note, then stuck it onto the murder wall next to the freeze-frame picture of the suspicious moped, "And the owner?"

"Yes Guv, a Mr DeAndre Phillips, 24 from East Ham. Lives in a flat off Lonsdale Avenue. He's had a few arrests for some low-level stuff. Burglary, possession, theft, that sort of thing."

"Are you sure Woody? Are you certain this is the right guy?"

"Yes," Woody sounded hurt. He turned his computer screen so everyone could see three separate pictures from the three different crime scenes. All showed the same moped with the same registration plate - HH56 SWM. Carson nodded, "Great work Oaks, really great work."

"Someone better alert MO19, right?" Hewson asked.

Carson glowered at her, then relented, "I'll make the call. Witz and Evans, get over to Lonsdale Avenue now and get eyeballs on the property. No heroics though, wait until we arrive with reinforcements."

"Yes Guv," the two detectives grabbed their jackets and rushed for the door.

"Hewson, call Chapman and give him an update. Tell him we're heading over to East Ham."

Misadvertised

Chapter Seventy-Three

Carson, Hewson and Oaks were in the Audi heading east when Evans called, "We're here Guv and we're in luck. The moped is parked out front of the flats."

Finally, something seemed to be going their way.

"Excellent, we'll be there in ten minutes with a Tactical Support Team to follow. Under no circumstances are you approach the suspect, do you understand?"

"Yes Guv."

Carson was thrumming with adrenaline. They all were. He switched to the in-car entertainment system and selected something loud and aggressive. *Rage Against The Machine*, Hewson guessed. Woody looked like his eardrums were about to burst. They drove without talking, lost in their own thoughts. *Probably just as well*, Hewson decided as her teeth began rattling.

Carson switched the music off again as they pulled into a small residential cul de sac, just off Lonsdale Avenue. An eight-storey block of nondescript flats rose above the enormous East Ham cemetery behind. Carson did a slow pass along the front of the building, noting Evans and Witz parked in a bay opposite the main entrance. He pulled up on a double yellow line where the road began to curve round behind the flats. From here they would be able to see if Phillips tried to escape through a rear exit.

A few minutes later a large unmarked van pulled into Lonsdale Close and turned right, pulling up next to a line of garages. Eight armed response officers leapt from the rear doors, clad all in black wearing bulletproof vests, helmets and balaclavas to protect their identity and clutching an automatic rifle. Immediately they split into two teams, four officers jogging quickly and quietly towards the front door, the other four headed for the rear of the building.

Carson twisted the dial on the top of his police radio, selecting the channel being used by the tactical support team, "I asked them not to shoot our suspect this time if at all possible."

"Bloody hell, did you really?" Hewson knew her boss was tactless, but even she was shocked.

"I did say please," he wasn't even being ironic.

The radio crackled into life.

"Alpha team entering building now."

"Copy Alpha One. Bravo team entering rear now."

There was a pause as the armed officers ran up the stairs, ensuring each landing was 'clear' as they passed.

"Ground floor, clear."

"First floor, clear."

"Second floor, clear."

"Third floor, clear."

"How do these guys do it?" Asked Woody, "I'm out of breath just listening to them."

"Fourth floor, clear."

"Breach! Breach! Breach!"

A few seconds later there were two very loud bangs, one after the other followed by the sound of splintering wood and several voices yelling, "Armed police! Stay where you are!"

"Did they just shoot the door off?" Hewson asked.

Carson nodded, "Two shotgun blasts to the door hinges. They are still angry about the Charlie Kingston thing."

There was an even louder bang that rattled the windows of all the flats in the block, a bright flash briefly illuminating the top floor windows.

"What the…?"

"Just a flash bang grenade," Carson interrupted, "Lots of light, lots of noise, limited damage too - assuming it doesn't land on you. Very effective at scaring the living daylights out of suspects. Or so I'm told."

The shouting and smashing continued for a few more minutes. The armed response team were either involved in a life-or-death struggle with the suspects, or taking great enjoyment from deconstructing DeAndre's flat. Eventually the noise quietened and a single voice came over the radio, "All clear, scene successfully secured. Three in custody. Repeat, three in custody."

"That's our cue," said Carson, jumping out of the car and jogging unsteadily towards the front entrance to the flats.

Chapter Seventy-Four

Woody wasn't the only one out of breath by the time the murder squad arrived on the fifth floor. Witz hadn't even bothered to try - he was waiting downstairs in the car. The others took a moment puffing and panting, trying to catch their breath before stepping over the splintered door and into flat 5C.

Looking at the scattered food packaging and assorted rubbish on the floor, it was obvious that Phillips wasn't particularly house proud. But the visiting MO19 officers had turned the apartment into a bomb site, with smashed glass and splintered furniture scattered everywhere.

"In here," a voice yelled from a doorway on the left of the hallway.

The room beyond was packed with burly, masked firearms officers quietly congratulating each other on a job well done. A huge flatscreen TV lay against the wall, glass splintered crazily from a direct blow, the unit it had been standing on was missing two legs, apparently the victim of another heavy booted kick. In amongst the wood splinters and shattered glass, three young black men lay face down on the floor, hands turning blue, zip-tied behind their backs. They must have really pissed off the armed response officers.

"DeAndre Phillips?" Carson asked.

Misadvertised

The man on the left mumbled, "Piss off pig."

"DeAndre Phillips, I am arresting you on suspicion of the murders of Paolo Nunez, Kirsten Grabowski, Ivan Yushenko and Stacey Kyle. You do not have to say anything, but anything you do say may be used in evidence against you. Do you understand?"

"Murder? What the hell? I never killed no one. Are you fitting me up? Bastard pigs!" He spat, writhing angrily on the floor.

"I'll take that as a 'yes'," Carson turned to the TST sergeant, "Could you gentlemen please bring Mr Phillips downstairs? Thanks ever so much."

Hewson surveyed the wreckage of the living room, "Evans and Woody, you two get to work searching this place. I'll give SOCO a call on the way back to BPR, get them over here to give you a hand. Assuming any evidence survived the armed assault."

Back downstairs, Hewson was less than amused to see Sherlock Homes walking across the grass, brandishing his smartphone and delivering a running commentary for the benefit of his livestream subscribers. She waved to a nearby uniformed officer, "Get a perimeter tape set up across here please. And make sure you keep the public outside the cordon until SOCO have cleared the area. Especially him."

Hewson pointed at Homes. The constable nodded, hurrying to intercept the would-be detective and hustling him back towards the car park where a small knot of other 'concerned citizens' were huddled, gawping, trying to capture the incident on camera for posterity. Or more likely, for 'Likes' on Facebook.

Misadvertised

"You've arrested the wrong guy again," Homes yelled at Hewson, "How many times are you going to keep making the same mistake?"

"Piss off Homes," the DS muttered, striding quickly towards the relative safety and solitude of Carson' car.

Chapter Seventy-Five

Reports coming in from East London suggest that Metropolitan Police have arrested one man and two accomplices in the hunt for the so-called 'Real Rock Restaurants Ripper'. The suspect has been named locally as DeAndre Phillips. Official Metropolitan Police sources have declined to comment but Mayor Carnt had this to say;
'I am delighted to hear that the police have a suspect in custody for these brutal murders and would like to thank them on behalf of all Londoners for their tireless efforts to bring the killer to justice. I am also thankful that the suspect was arrested without the use of force and that we have not seen a repeat of the over-zealous behaviour which resulted in the tragic shooting of a young immigrant woman this morning.'"

"What a *bastard*," Hewson muttered.

Chapter Seventy-Six

Carson and Hewson watched DeAndre talking with the duty solicitor through the one-way window. The young man was clearly agitated, his long thin arms gesturing wildly. With the intercom switched off, Carson could only assume he was protesting his innocence.

"It's not him," Carson sighed, exasperated.

"We haven't even spoken to the guy yet," Hewson said, "He still looks good for this."

"It wasn't him," Carson shook his head, "Look. He's pissing himself with fear."

"Maybe he's just frightened of having to face the consequences of his actions?" Hewson suggested.

"No, he's panicking about being jammed up for something he *didn't* do."

After a few minutes of slightly less animated discussion, the solicitor was finally able to calm his client. He waved at the window to indicate they were ready to begin the interview.

"OK, here we go," Hewson took a deep breath and followed Carson into the room.

Sat in a prison issue grey sweatshirt, DeAndre was clearly still agitated. The humiliation of having your clothes and personal belongings taken away during a strip search tends to do that to a person. Carson sat down at the table opposite DeAndre and stared at the young man for a few moments.

Eventually he pressed the red button on the desktop interview recorder and began the interrogation.

"This interview is being tape recorded and may be given in evidence if your case is brought to trial. We are in an interview room at Balls Pond Road Police Station. The date is Monday, the 27th February 2023 and the time by my watch is 1509 hours. I am Detective Inspector James Carson. Also present is…"

He paused to allow Hewson to fill in the blank, "Detective Sergeant Leyla Hewson."

"Please state your full name and date of birth," he nodded to DeAndre.

"DeAndre Lionel Michael Phillips. 19th January 2000," the young man mumbled.

"Also present is…"

"Mr Andrew Mink, duty solicitor."

"So DeAndre, do you agree that there are no other persons present?"

DeAndre nodded without lifting his eyes from the table.

"I need you to say it for the tape please."

Obviously tapes had been replaced by digital audio recorders but old habits, and turns of speech, die hard.

"Yes," DeAndre mumbled again.

"OK, now before we go any further, I need to remind you that you are under caution. This means that you do not have to say anything, but it may harm your defence if you do not mention when questioned something you later rely on in court. Anything you do say may be given in evidence. Do you understand."

"Yes," DeAndre muttered again.

Carson placed his notebook on the table and began to scribble, "You have been arrested on suspicion of murder, DeAndre. Four murders in fact. So I need you to tell me where you were on Tuesday night."

"I already told you, I never killed no one," some of DeAndre's belligerence had returned.

"Yes, you did. But you're still going to have to convince my colleague, DS Hewson here. So let's start at the beginning - where were you on the night of Tuesday 21st February DeAndre?"

The young man looked at his brief who gave him a small, almost imperceptible nod.

"I was meeting a guy over in Greenwich."

"Yeah? Greenwich is a bit out of your area DeAndre. Who were you meeting?"

"Bloke calls himself Nicky Ninebar. Dunno what his real name is. We were hanging out at the NG Speakeasy."

"Is that the one in Greenwich?" Hewson clarified.

"Yeah," DeAndre nodded, "Apparently the bastard only does business at night. I didn't get out until the sun was coming up."

"And what did Nicky Ninebar want from a low-level wideboy like you?"

DeAndre looked at his brief who gave a tiny shake of the head.

"No comment."

Scribble, scribble, scribble.

"OK, we'll come back to that. What about Wednesday the 22nd?"

"Just out and about, innit."

"Out and about *where?*"

"Out and about in the city, riding my bike."

"You're going to have to be more specific than that DeAndre," Carson said giving him a steely look, "Where in the city? Who was with you?"

"Just out riding in East London with a couple of my boys. The ones you grabbed when you shot the door off my flat. They'll back me up."

"Of course they will. Did anyone else see you?"

"No," DeAndre looked away.

"Fine. And on the morning of Friday the 24th?"

"Morning? I was in bed man," DeAndre seemed shocked that anyone would willing rise before midday.

"Alone?"

"Yeah."

Carson pretended to look at his notes, "So Tuesday you were meeting with a known drug dealer. Wednesday you were 'out and about' on your bike. Friday morning, you were home alone. Is that correct."

"Yeah," DeAndre nodded, he seemed to be becoming more confident, "And like I keep telling you, I never killed no-one."

Hewson cut in, "Stop pissing us about DeAndre. Let's start by you telling us what you were really doing on Wednesday night. Perhaps these photos will help jog your memory." She spread several large, full colour crime scene prints of the four murder victims across the top of the table.

DeAndre went another shade paler, looked like he was going to puke.

"Seriously man, what the hell?" He pushed the pictures back towards Leyla, "I told you I ain't killed no one. This is some sick shit and you ain't gonna pin it on me."

"So where were you on Wednesday night?"

DeAndre stared at her angrily for a moment, then sighed, "Me n fam were down Shoreditch nicking phones."

"Explain," said Carson.

"We watch them hipsters walking down the road playing on their phones. Ride up behind them, snatch the handset, ride off. Pocket the iPhones, bin the Androids. Wash, rinse, repeat. Even easier now you can rent them dumb bikes and escooters on every street corner. Most of those dickheads wear big headphones, can't even hear you coming. "

"So when was this happening?"

"'Til about 10, then we went back to East Ham."

"For?"

"Sell the phones. Have to get rid of them quick before hipster guy gets home and deactivates his missing iPhone."

"Who do you sell them to?"

"No chance mate, I ain't giving you no name. Not while you think I killed four people."

"One of your 'fam' is bound to give us the name eventually DeAndre, so you should probably get in quick while I'm feeling generous. Maybe I can put in a good word for you when you're charged with the mobile phone robberies."

Misadvertised

DeAndre looked at his solicitor who gave him a tiny nod. "Guy called Techy Tony," he said with a defeated sigh, "He works for the Turks. A real bad ass called Sahin."

"Techy Tony," repeated Carson, scribbling the name in his pad, "And where can we find this Mr Tony?"

"He runs a phone repair shop down on the Barking Road, next door to a dodgy nail salon. Flogs off the iPhones under the counter," DeAndre lowered his voice, "Whatever you do, keep my name out of it. Sahin is a dangerous bastard and I have to live on his turf. He would kill me if he knew I had been speaking with Nicky Ninebar. Or you."

"I'll see what I can do, but I have no interest in your petty gang squabbles and shifting loyalties," Carson nodded at the window. Behind the two-way mirror, Witz headed for the door to go and speak with Techy Tony.

Chapter Seventy-Seven

Carson had paused the interview not long after DeAndre had given up the name of Techy Tony. He already knew in his gut that the young phone thief's alibis would check out, that DeAndre would soon move off the suspect list. Carson and Hewson stood in the corridor drinking coffee from the vending machine - or as he liked to call it, 'mud'.

"Do you want me to go and speak to Nicky Ninebar?" Hewson asked.

"No, let's wait and see what Techy Tony says to Witz first," the DI replied, shaking his head, "DeAndre is telling us the truth."

"You were right," Hewson nodded.

Carson wandered back into his squad's open plan office and stared at the murder wall for a moment. If this was a game, he already had all the pieces of the puzzle. The problem was that the pieces just would not fit together. He was still scratching his head when his mobile rang.

"Bad news Guv," it was Witz, "Techy Tony confirms that DeAndre *was* here late on Wednesday night. He even coughed to the stolen iPhones, had a whole box of them under the counter. Shall I nick him?"

Misadvertised

"No, pass it over to Whitechapel CID, they have a team looking into smartphone thefts. Come back to the station so we can regroup and decide what to do next."

He dialled Evans, "What have you found out about DeAndre's movements on Friday?"

"Phillips has a video doorbell so I checked the footage. He's seen entering his property in the early hours of Friday morning and he doesn't leave again until 14:23 that afternoon. I also checked with a neighbour whose front door faces the stairs and lifts. DeAndre definitely did not leave his flat that morning. Not unless he jumped out of a rear window."

"On the fourth floor? Not bloody likely. Get yourself back to BPR DC Evans."

"Ballbags," said Hewson, as Carson unpinned DeAndre's mugshot from the murder wall.

Misadvertised

Chapter Seventy-Eight

Carson was heading back to the shed when his phone rang. It was Chapman.

"Hello Guv, everything ok?"

"No, it's not. I think I have another body for your collection," the Chief Super's voice boomed in his ear.

"Another Real Rock murder?"

"Not sure yet, you'll have to tell me. Remember the sewer guy, Barry Green? The one who went looking for golems with Witz? He's dead."

"Right...?"

"At first the SOCO thought he'd died in an accident. Looks like the silly bastard fell and broke his neck somewhere in the tunnels. His body was carried all the way out into the Thames past Blackfriars. They found him in one of those crap collectors designed to trap rubbish floating in the river."

"Right...?"

"Yes, the reason I thought you may want to take a look is because he was tangled up in a bag."

"A black and red rucksack?"

"That's the one. I've arranged for it to be sent to forensics."

"Perfect, thanks Guv."

Misadvertised

"Uniform assumed it was a suicide so they arranged for the body to be transported before I was made aware of the discovery. Because they pull a jumper out of the river at least once a week, they thought Barry was just another one. Sorry about that."

"To be fair, I'd probably have done the same," Carson agreed, "And if Barry really was killed by our man and dumped somewhere else, I doubt there would have been much useful evidence in the crap catcher anyway. I'll chase up forensics in the morning, then make a decision about whether Mr Green is part of our investigation. Night Guv."

Carson hung up the call and let himself into the shed, scanning the small space sorrowfully. Never in his life had he imagined he would be sharing a bed with a lawnmower instead of Eva. He was pleased to see there was a plate of cold food waiting for him on the workbench tonight, some kind of pea and ham soup with hard crusty bread. His tummy rumbled with appreciation. Despite being chilled, the food was tasty and he was sincerely grateful for something to eat.

Carson sent Eva a quick text to share his gratitude, *Dinner was great. Thank you!* He paused for a moment, then sent a follow up, *I love you*. He was pleased to see the little 'Read' notification below his message, even if his wife didn't send a reply.

Soup finished, he switched off the light, settled back into the sleeping bag and stared into the darkness. Sleep wouldn't come however, so he reached for his iPhone and began scrolling Wikipedia looking for more useless trivia with which to distract himself. Hopefully he would find something to impress Shaw at the next pub quiz.

Misadvertised

#

The River Fleet is the largest of London's subterranean rivers, all of which today contain foul water for treatment. It has been used as a sewer since the development of Joseph Balzagette's London sewer system in the mid-19th century...

Chapter Seventy-Nine

"Well viewers, it's been a *massive* day in the Real Rock Restaurant Ripper case. We started this morning with the shooting of a potential suspect who it turns out wasn't actually a suspect at all. In a disturbing case of mistaken identity, a young woman was shot by some very enthusiastic officers from the Met Police's armed division, MO19."

Homes was hyped, arms windmilling as if the speed and size of gestures would help to transmit his enthusiasm to his channel subscribers.

"But my sources tell me that the young woman is actually an illegal immigrant who shares a fake identity, Charlie Kingston, with several other illegals, allowing them to pick up work as delivery drivers for the FeedMeNow app. Apparently Charlie Kingston was present at all three Real Rock Restaurants on the same date as each murder. It just wasn't the *same* Charlie Kingston each time."

Footage of the shooting, clearly captured on a mobile phone, began to play onscreen. The moped rider pulled up on the pavement and began unloading food from the delivery box mounted behind the pillion. The rider is then surrounded by masked gunmen, shouting loudly to get face down on the ground. The rider continues unloading oblivious. Eventually a plain clothes detective lumbers into the field of view yelling at the armed officers to stand down. There's the crack of a shot and the rider stumbles backwards and falls to the pavement.

The footage restarts, this time playing at half speed while Homes provides his own observations, "As you can see, the rider simply does not hear the instructions through their crash helmet. When this unknown officer runs into the fray," Homes points at Carson who is only visible from behind, "someone panics and opens fire. Fortunately, the young woman is going to be fine. And I hear she has also been ruled out as a suspect."

"But the action didn't stop there, oh no!" Homes is windmilling again, "This afternoon, the murder squad took their chances with MO19 again, this time kicking in the door of one DeAndré Phillips, whose moped had been spotted at each of the murder scenes. Thankfully, the raid finished without any significant injuries."

A picture of a battered and lightly bleeding DeAndré being bundled into the back of a Police van flashed up on screen.

"But guess what? The murder squad went two-for-two after Mr Phillips was able to successfully alibi himself!"

Homes made a sarcastic *mwah-mwah-mwah-mwaaaaah* trumpet sound to indicate the failure.

"It's not all bad though. Mr Phillips' alibi was that he and his accomplices were busy stealing iPhones in East London on Wednesday, leaving them too busy to kill anyone. So the detectives may not have managed to catch the Real Rock Restaurant Ripper," a picture of Max

Jackson flashed up on screen, "But they *did* bust a smartphone robbery ring. So I guess that's a kind of win."

Cue applause sound effect.

"Obviously all this excitement has had some significant effects on the Real Rock Ripper Gaming Room odds. At one point our favourite Max Jackson was as high as 15 to 1 when the finger started pointing elsewhere but now he's fallen back to 1 to 2…"

"Anyway, it's been a big day. Can the Met top it tomorrow? Fingers crossed…!"

Misadvertised

Chapter Eighty

Hewson was walking in another packed Real Rock Restaurant, weaving between tables and using her elbows to make her way through the crowd gathered at the bar. Despite the pushing and jostling, she felt light, her feet floated a few inches above the floor.

The crowd was laughing and joking, people having a good time, but Hewson felt entirely disconnected from them - and her emotions. She was scanning the walls, taking in each display case and the item of musical history contained therein.

Drumsticks used by Keith Moon, *quick stab through the eyes*. Maracas owned by Mick Jagger, *slow, noisy, painful battering*. Stone bust from the Sergeant Pepper's Lonely Hearts Club Band album cover, *dropped on head, from height*. David Bowie's belt, *garrotte*. Assorted gold discs, *fatal frisbees*.

Dream Hewson paused. Not only was she identifying potential murder weapons, she was also imagining how they may be used, the gorier the better. Every item she looked at was imbued with lethal potential, her imagination creating shocking and fatal injuries with surprising ease. She realised she was scanning the tables looking for potential victims, visualising the carnage, the blood, the sheer violence. And she was *enjoying* the feeling.

Misadvertised

Dream Hewson hacked and slashed, strangled, mutilated and crushed while the diners around her remained oblivious to the carnage unfolding around them. Each face was an indistinct blur until it was their time to die, suddenly morphing into a twisted scream of terror and pain. Each time she struck it was David's face that she saw contorted in horror, staring up at her.

The blood from her victims pooled on the restaurant floor, lapping over the top of her shoes, soaking her socks and trouser cuffs. It was warm and sticky and surprisingly welcoming. She considered laying down in the crimson tide, bathing in the blood of her victims, absorbing their life force.

Thoughts of reclining in the warm river of red evaporated were interrupted by a banging on the restaurant window. Moments later a giant avenging angel clad in black leather strode through the door, his enormous bulk filling the doorway, helmeted head and feathered wingtips scraping on the ceiling above. The angel spoke but all she heard was the rumbling of thunder. She shook her head and pointed at her ears and shrugged. The black celestial creature called out again but she still couldn't understand what it was saying.

The beast shrugged, withdrawing a large flaming sword from the scabbard strapped to his belt. He pointed it at Hewson, releasing a blinding white ball of fire from the blade that struck her in the chest, throwing her off her feet. She howled in agony as her body splashed onto the floor, inhaling a mouthful of the thick warm blood. She coughed and choked and died.

This damn case is killing me.

Misadvertised

Chapter Eighty-One

There had been no murders for a few days, so Kevin Wu was confident the killings were over - or at least that's what he told his mother when he left for his shift at the Real Rock Restaurant in Waterloo. It had been another relatively busy night compared to the previous month and he had to admit that the 'Ripper' had certainly helped to boost footfall - and profits. For the first time in over a year their had been talk about hiring more people. Not only were the tables full but there were so many would-be diners waiting that they had had to reintroduce their old queuing system.

The last couple of diners had left just before midnight and his team of waiters had followed shortly afterwards, once the tables had been cleaned and the dishwasher loaded and reloaded. Wu just needed to finish restocking the bar and he would be free to go home too. He turned the incessant rock soundtrack down to a more bearable level, and finally he could hear himself think.

Kevin had just returned from the stock room with an armful of bottles and plonked them on the bar when he heard a noise coming from the corner of the room, by the sweeping glass staircase that led to the atrium above. He laughed, perhaps he wasn't completely 'over' the fear of being murdered at work yet.

Misadvertised

He quickly stopped laughing when a masked figure rose swiftly out of the shadows and smashed a bottle of gin over his head. He almost stopped breathing when the man hit him again with a second bottle. He collapsed to the ground amid the shards of shattered glass and spilled liquor.

Kevin became aware of the throbbing in his head as he began to slide back into consciousness. He was wet, it was dark and he could hear someone grunting with physical effort. It took him a few moments to realise he was still at work. In the dark. Bent over Elvis Presley's gold grand piano, the centre piece of his restaurant's memorabilia display.

A moment later Kevin wished he'd never woken up as the lid of the piano came crashing down on his head. Unfortunately it took another three agonising blows before the eternal darkness swallowed him up.

Chapter Eighty-Two

Sherlock Homes was waiting for the detectives outside the Real Rock Restaurant, camera poised to capture their arrival. "I knew you had the wrong man," he crowed triumphantly, "You've got a guy in custody and then there's another murder. Ergo, you have the wrong man."

"Piss off Homes," Hewson said.

"Ah, DS Hewson, thank you" he smiled, giving her a mock salute, "I owe you something for bringing so much traffic to my YouTube channel. How about a tip to help you solve this case? It was Jackson."

"Piss off Homes," she said again, louder this time.

Carson pushed the door of the restaurant open and Homes elbowed his way through the crowd, sucked under the cordon tape and made to follow the detectives inside. Hewson gave him a hefty shove in the chest, *"Piss off Homes."*

At first the amateur detective looked like he was going to cry, then he thought better of it, pressing his phone up against the glass door so that he could film the detectives moving around inside. Hewson gave him the finger, then sent a uniformed officer outside to move him along.

Shaw was waiting inside, hopping from foot to foot like he was excited about something.

Misadvertised

"Definitely a case of *Love Me Tender*-ised," Hewson couldn't see his mouth, but Shaw's comically arched eyebrows showed he was grinning somewhere below his mask. He was standing next to a tacky gold-leafed grand piano that was now covered in blood, splintered bone and grey squidgy stuff that Hewson assumed was brain matter. A large sign beside the instrument displayed a picture of a grinning Elvis Presley standing by the piano in Graceland.

"Now *that* was a good one," Carson nodded appreciatively.

"Please don't," Hewson groaned.

"*Don't*. Number two in 1958. Very well played DS Hewson," Shaw nodded appreciatively. Hewson groaned again, "Please, no more."

"Wow, an album track, Blue Hawaii I think," the SOCO was impressed, "Are you an Elvis fan, Hewson?"

"I'm leaving" she turned on her heel and walked over to the bar.

"*I'm Leavin'*, ha ha ha!" Shaw was laughing so hard he began to cough, "*You Gotta Stop* Hewson, you're killing me ha ha ha. You know we have an opening on our music quiz team? What are you doing Friday night?"

When he finally caught his breath, Carson steered his focus back towards the victim, "So what do we have Derek?"

"All I can tell you is that the vic is male and the cause of death was almost certainly blunt force trauma."

"Almost certainly?"

"Well the poor guy's head has been completely pulped, so it's possible something else happened and the killer smashed his skull to hide the evidence. We're going to have to scoop what's left out of the piano and take it to the morgue in a bucket. But for now it looks like the killer incapacitated him over there," he pointed at the smashed bottles on the floor by the bar, "then dragged the unconscious victim over here." A slimy, sticky trail of gin snaked across the floor to the piano.

"And do we have a name?"

"Kevin Wu, general manager. By the way, you're still yellow apart from your fingers which are turning blue."

"Thanks mate, you always say the nicest things," Carson replied, finishing his scribbling and pocketing his notebook.

"I'm serious James you're sick - and getting sicker every time I see you. You need to see a doctor. Today."

"A couple of aspirin and I'll be fine," he muttered, launching into a coughing fit. When he regained his breath, he weaved away from the body, heading towards Hewson, "Anything else of note? Have you found the Killer's message?"

"Nope, there's nothing. Something is different. Something is 'wrong' if that's the right word."

"Well there's no bloody message for a start," Carson said. He fished out his smartphone and jabbed at the screen for a few moments, "Hmmmmmm…"

Misadvertised

Chapter Eighty-Three

Back at the Balls Pond Road, Carson pinned a picture of Kevin Wu to the murder wall. They really needed to catch this guy quickly, not least because he had run out of wall space.

"OK, two things from me," Carson addressed his team loudly, "First, DeAndre Phillips' alibis for the other murders checked out, so we cut him loose this morning. Second, we have another victim, Kevin Wu aged 26, murdered at the Real Rock Restaurant in Waterloo last night. Blunt force trauma. Everywhere."

He pinned a picture of the bloodied crime scene under Kevin's portrait. His body propped against the side of the piano, blood and brain matter splattered down the golden woodwork, pooling on the floor below.

"Bloody hell," Evans exclaimed.

"Yup, everywhere," Carson nodded. He examined the murder wall and removed DeAndre's mugshot along with the sticky note and the numberplate Oaks had spotted yesterday.

"Sorry about that boss," the young DC mumbled.

"Don't apologise Woody, it was a good call," said Witz, patting him on the shoulder, "Not your fault the suspect is using fake plates."

"Late last night I took a call from Chief Superintendent Chapman," Carson announced, "That guy you went spelunking in the sewers with...?"

"Barry," Witz croaked.

"Yes, Barry. His body washed up in the Thames yesterday. It looked like an accident, body had been smashed about in the water, but he was tangled up in a black and red rucksack."

Carson pinned a picture of thin, brown-haired man onto the wall in the 'victim' section, before drawing a question mark beside the name, *Barry Green*.

"Bloody hell," Evans commented, "What are the odds of that? Is he a victim of our killer? What do you reckon Witz?"

Witz shook his head.

"The Chief Super put a rush on the forensics on the bag," Carson continued, "Unfortunately it didn't take long to complete their magic tests because there was nothing to find. Just excrement from half of London's residents soaked through the fabric."

"Lovely," said Woody, "So is Barry linked to this case, or is it just a freaky coincidence?"

Witz let out a sigh.

"You ok mate?" Evans asked her partner, ignoring Woody, "You don't look so good."

"You wouldn't either if you'd been the one sent to wade through knee-high sewerage looking for an imaginary Jewish clay monster," Witz snapped.

"Now then children," Carson turned back to face his colleagues and stumbled off-balance by a sudden dizzy spell. He dropped his handful of pictures and notes on the floor, steadying himself with a hand on a nearby desk.

"Are you alright Guv?" Hewson asked, concerned.

Carson didn't move. He continued to stare at the floor. The team exchanged worried glances.

"Guv?"

"Oaks, what was the number plate on the CCTV footage?"

Woody scrabbled around his desk, sifting through scraps of paper. "Erm, HH56 SWM," he read from his pad.

Carson bent down and retrieved the dropped sticky note. "Humour me for a moment," he muttered, standing upright once more, "Do a reg check on WM59 SHH."

Woody pecked away at his keyboard for a few seconds, "WM59 SHH. It's a moped belonging to a Mr Julian Thorn of Notting Hill. Works for the Browning-Hughes-Khan investment bank in The City, no priors."

"So what does Julian Thorn have to do with anything?" Asked Evans.

Carson held up the sticky note bearing the registration number, "What does it say?"

"HH56 SWM," Evans said, puzzled. Carson rotated the piece of paper 180 degrees.

"What does it say now?"

"WM59 SHH," she read, "That's really clever."

"If our Mr Julian Thorn has anything to do with the murders, that's really arrogant. So , assuming no one else has any decent leads, Hewson and I are going to interview him."

Misadvertised

Chapter Eighty-Four

Carson was in a foul mood by the time they had crawled through traffic to the offices of Browning-Hughes Khan. The dizziness had eased, only to be replaced by a crushing pain in the top of his skull. Probably not quite as painful as being battered to death with a grand piano he reasoned, but it was still bloody uncomfortable. Hewson had tried to talk to him about what was going on but he had waved her concern away.

Rather than circle the block endlessly looking for a parking spot that didn't exist, Carson simply abandoned his car at the front door of the Browning-Hughes-Khan building. Hewson thought that was an incredible risk - she half expected them to finish speaking with Mr Julian Thorn and come back to find the vehicle towed away and destroyed by anti-terrorism officers.

Carson didn't wait to hear her concerns, instead barrelling through the revolving glass door and into the steel and granite reception area. The building had been designed to showcase the vast wealth of the Browning-Hughes-Khan Bank with an atrium that extended seven storeys above street level. Stainless steel and glass walkways crisscrossed the atrium, power suited men and women scuttling to and fro like a collection of grey ants.

Misadvertised

The overall impression was one of supreme confidence and obscene wealth.

Hewson caught up with Carson who was already haranguing the receptionist, "Julian Thorn, where is he?"

Despite looking not a day over fifteen, the young man was a pro, "Mr Thorn works in our risk analysis division. Do you have an appointment sir?"

"Yes," Carson growled, "Show him your badge, Hewson."

Hewson dutifully flashed her warrant card along with an apologetic shrug and half-smile. The receptionist squinted at the badge and tapped at his keyboard for a moment. As if by magic, a dark suited security man appeared from a door behind the reception desk and stepped forward to greet the detectives. He nodded curtly to them both, then indicated that they should follow him as he strode purposefully towards one of the glass-fronted elevators that shuttled continuously between floors. Once inside, he waved his ID badge at a small pad below the buttons then pressed the one numbered '6'.

When the door opened, the man stepped out with the same purposeful gait. He waved his entry card at another panel and a large glass door slid open soundlessly, revealing a huge, dimly-lit open plan office. The area was subdivided by what looked like hundreds of cubicles, each staffed by a single person working under an angle poise lamp. The only sound was the murmur of hushed voices and one hundred computer keyboards being pummelled simultaneously.

The guard continued striding between the cubicles, eventually stopping next to a desk about three-quarters of

Misadvertised

the way down the room. He whispered something to the cubicle occupant, then stepped back and nodded. The man stood up to face them, grinning, "Officers! I am Julian Thorn. Before we begin, can I please ask if the purpose of your visit is professional or personal?"

Hewson recognised the well-dressed young man, but she couldn't quite place the face.

Carson was taken aback, "The Metropolitan Police are not in the habit of making visits 'for fun'."

"Oh no. No, no, no," the man shook his head, "I was simply asking whether you were investigating a matter related to Browning-Hughes-Khan Bank or to me personally. If your questions are business related, I am contractually obligated to have in-house counsel present."

"Oh," Carson mumbled, the man's affability was unusual - and disconcerting, "I'm DI Carson and this is DS Hewson. We're here to see you personally Mr Thorn. Nothing to do with your job."

"Good, good," Thorn said, nodding and smiling, "If you would like to follow me, we can talk in one of the meeting rooms. Much quieter in there."

Hewson smiled, this was the quietest office she had ever seen. The man led them to the far side of the open-plan office and through another glass door. Inside, a large polished wood conference table dominated the space, eclipsed only by the wall-to-ceiling window that looked out over the steel and glass skycap of the City of London. Thorn waved Hewson and Carson to take a seat, "Can I offer you a drink? Tea? Coffee? Water?"

"No thank you Mr Thorn," the DI said, "We just have a few questions and then we'll be out of your way."

"Fine," the man smiled again. "You're staring at me DS Hewson. Trying to remember where you've seen me before perhaps?"

Hewson flushed and nodded slightly.

"No need to be embarrassed," Thorn laughed easily, "We passed each other in Dr Jenkins' office the day before yesterday."

Of course, the well-dressed, shy young man in the therapist's waiting room.

"So, shall we make a start?" Thorn reached for a small silver box that looked like a television remote control. Pressing a red button, the glass dividing wall frosted and the office behind disappeared, "Now we can continue without being disturbed. Are you here about the Real Rock Restaurant murders?"

Chapter Eighty-Five

For some reason, this guy had an uncanny ability to throw Carson off his stride.

Hewson took over, "Yes we are, Mr Thorn. Do you know something about the murders?"

"Absolutely I do," he nodded, smiling broadly, "I am the man you're looking for."

Carson and Hewson exchanged glances. Neither of them had expected to elicit a confession.

"You do understand what you are saying, Mr Thorn?"

"Oh yes," he nodded, his smile getting broader.

Carson shrugged, "In that case, Julian Thorn I am arresting you on suspicion of the murders of Paolo Nunez, Kirsten Grabowski, Ivan Yusheno, Stacey Kyle, Barry Green and Kevin Wu. You do not have to say anything, but anything you do say can and will be used against you in court. Do you understand?"

"Well yes and no," Thorn had stopped smiling and now looked confused, "Who are Barry Green and Kevin Wu?"

"We'll get into that back at the police station Mr Thorn," Hewson replied, reaching for her cuffs, "Now if you wouldn't mind accompanying us..."

"On no, there's no need for that detective," Thorn said, "I'll come quietly."

Misadvertised

"I know you will," she answered, "In cuffs."
There was no way she going anywhere with an unshackled serial killer, no matter how sweetly he smiled.

Misadvertised

Chapter Eighty-Six

Chapman stood with his arms folded across his chest, staring through the one-way mirror at Julian Thorn sat in the interview room, "And just like that, he confessed?"

"Yes," Carson nodded, "Puzzling eh?"

"Is he on a wind-up?"

"Nope," said Hewson, "He's very convincing."

"OK," Chapman sighed, "Have at it then."

"Oaks," Carson said to his DC, "Can you have forensics run biometric profiling across the murder footage? Get them to compare Thorn with the CCTV images to see if we can get a match."

"Will do Guv," the young man said, scurrying off.

Carson nodded to Chapman, then led Hewson into the interview room. As before, they seated themselves at the desk, started the interview recorder and reminded Julian Thorn he was under caution. With the formalities out of the way, Carson stared at their suspect. The man stared back, studying the DI with undisguised curiosity.

Eventually Hewson broke the silence, "Are you sure you don't want legal representation Mr Thorn? I can arrange to have the duty solicitor speak with you if you can't afford your own representation."

"Oh no, no," the man said, "That really won't be necessary. I'd like to re-state for the record, I murdered

Misadvertised

Paolo Nunez, Kirsten Grabowski, Ivan Yushenko and Stacey Kyle."

"And Kevin Wu?"

"No, I'm afraid that wasn't me detective," the man shook his head mournfully, "My message had been received and Real Rock Restaurants responded appropriately. There was no need for anyone else to die."

"Right then, let's start at the beginning," said Carson, "Do you own a moped with the registration WM59 SHH?"

"Yes," Thorn winked, "Out of interest, how long did you spend looking for the rider of HH5 SWM?"

"Long enough to take down a network of smartphone thieves, Mr Thorn," Hewson said, "But if your ruse was so clever, why not choose a completely different registration?"

"Just one of those weird patterns that my brain latches onto I guess. Unfortunately most people miss these beautiful, random patterns in unexpected places. I couldn't resist sharing it."

"Beautiful. Great," Carson cut in, "Where were you on the night of Tuesday the 21st February between 10pm and 2am?"

"I was at the Greenwich Real Rock Restaurant. But I actually arrived much earlier and hung around with the delivery drivers. 'Casing the joint' as they like to call it."

"Only when 'they' are planning a burglary," Hewson muttered, "In the case of murder *we* call it 'premeditation'."

"Yes, of course. Premeditation," Julian Thorn nodded, "I should add that I stopped on the way home to burn my hazmat suit, gloves, mask, goggles, backpack, the lot. I turned everything to ash."

"Of course. And what about Wednesday 22nd?" Carson prompted.

"Camden, obviously. It was there that I strangled Kirsten. Then I dropped my bag of evidence down a manhole into the sewers before I went home for a shower."

"And the morning of Friday 24th?"

"Battering Ivan and Stacey to death. I had to take lunch early that day to make sure I got to Soho before the restaurant opened. And I had to take a risk, throwing the evidence into the Thames on the way back to work. I would have preferred to burn it, but we all know what happened last time there was a fire in the City of London."

"You do know Stacey wasn't actually dead?"

"Yes, I heard. She must have suffered greatly. That was awful."

The man was calm, collected and completely open, almost like he wanted to help the detectives get the case wrapped up quickly. Hewson found his demeanour more disturbing than the usual wife-beaters and drunks and pathetic teenage gang members their team normally dealt with.

"And what about Sunday 26th?"

"Sunday? I was up about nine, went for a run in the park. I went over to my parents' house in Holland Park for lunch around 1pm and stayed all afternoon. Then I had a session with Dr Jenkins, my therapist, between six and seven. Following his advice, I had another run in the park before heading home around 10pm and in bed shortly before 11pm."

Julian Thorn sat back in his chair and smiled.

Misadvertised

"And you didn't leave the house again?" Hewson asked.

"No," a shake of the head.

"Did you go to Waterloo at any point on Sunday?"

"No, detective," another shake of the head, "I didn't even go south of the River that day."

"What about Barry Green? Did you kill him on Saturday or Sunday?"

"Barry who?" for the first time Thorn looked unsure of himself.

"Barry was the man in the sewers. The one who found your carefully disposed of rucksack."

"Sorry detective, I have no idea what you are talking about."

"So you're confessing to the murders of Paolo Nunez, Kirsten Grabowski, Ivan Yushenko and Stacey Kyle but you're denying responsibility for the murders of Barry Green and Kevin Wu. Why?" Asked Carson.

"Because I didn't kill Barry or Kevin. It wasn't me," Julian Thorn smiled, "Paolo, Kirsten, Ivan and Stacey were the unfortunate collateral when Real Rock Restaurants began the slide into misadvertising."

Hewson raised an eyebrow, "'Collateral'? How so?"

Thorn nodded at Carson, "He knows. He got the message. He even wrote in on your case board out there in the office."

"The soundtrack," Carson answered, "When Real Rock Restaurants started stuffing their playlist with pop music and rap, you were offended."

Misadvertised

"Not offended as such, but certainly disappointed at the way the brand misrepresented, *misadvertised*, itself," Thorn said with a wink.

"Is that even a real word?" Carson hit back.

"It is now," Thorn smiled again, "You certainly won't forget it in a hurry."

"Wait, I don't get it. You killed four, maybe five, people just because a restaurant plays what you call 'the wrong music'?" Hewson couldn't believe this was a genuine motive.

"No DS Hewson, I don't say it is the wrong music," Julian Thorn shook his head, "It's not *rock* music - which is what RRR is supposed to be all about. It's right there in the name of the business. It's printed on all the t-shirts and badges and glasses and ephemera that they flog to their customers in the gift shop."

"So you were going to keep killing people until RRR management got the message and changed their in-store soundtrack so it only played 'true' rock music. Why didn't you just send a letter of complaint.

"Oh I did, detective," the man nodded sadly, "Only no one took any notice. I suspect they didn't even read them. So I had to send a bloodier message. One that they could not ignore."

"Bloody hell," Hewson muttered under her breath.

"Sometimes you have to be blunt," Thorn continued, "And someone has to stand up for what is right - even on seemingly trivial matters like music playlists."

"And murdering people was just a natural aspect of this crusade for truth?" Carson asked.

"Well, Dr Jenkins says that I can quickly become obsessive. My unfortunate ability to see matters in black and white makes me super-sensitive to these issues when they occur. And so I feel I must take action to right the wrongs - even if those actions seem extreme."

Hewson stared at Thorn. He was quite, quite mad. There was a tap on the door and Chapman stuck his head into the interview room and gestured that the detectives should follow.

"Interview paused at 16:28," Carson said for the benefit of the recorder. "You, stay here," he barked at Thorn, then walked out of the room to speak with Chapman.

Chapter Eighty-Seven

"What the actual *f...*" Chapman began, once the door to the interview room was closed.

"I know, I know," Carson cut him off, "But we have a confession from a verified suspect."

"Verified nut job you mean," Chapman was agitated and angry, "Is this some kind of build-up to a diminished capacity defence? Is Thorn going to claim he not mentally fit to face trial?"

"Honestly? I doubt it. Although he doesn't see anything wrong with what he's done, he does seem willing to pay the price for his actions," Carson shook his head, "And thankfully he doesn't have a solicitor to lay the groundwork for a defence like that."

"Should we speak to Dr Jenkins?" Hewson asked.

"I'm not sure we're going to need to," Carson shook his head, "Think about it - in addition to Thorn's confession, we have CCTV footage of him in the restaurants, and on his moped in the vicinity of each murder within the right timeframes. We have a motive, twisted and deranged as it may be, and we know that he had opportunity."

"Do we have any forensics to tie him to the scenes? Anything at all?" Chapman asked, "Witz is overseeing a search of Thorn's flat but he's found nothing. And it will take months for IT to complete a trawl of his computer and smartphone."

Oaks came rushing down the corridor towards them, "Forensics have done a preliminary comparison against the footage from all four murder scenes. They kept stressing that they needed to conduct some more in-depth tests, but at the moment, Thorn is a 92.8% biometric fit for Greenwich, Camden and Soho based on height and gait."

"Yes!" Chapman hissed.

"Hold on," Carson raised a hand to calm his boss, "What about Waterloo?"

"They reckon only 67% on that one," Woody nodded, "Something about the way the perp walks. Either Thorn's really good at faking or, more likely, it's not him at all."

"Big sweaty balls," Hewson exclaimed in frustration, "So what does that mean? Thorn has an accomplice?"

"No," Carson shook his head again, "Thorn said he had completed what he set out to do. I think we're looking for a copycat."

There was a *tap-tap-tap* on the two way mirror. Thorn was beckoning them back into the interview room.

Chapter Eighty-Eight

"Have you figured it out yet detectives?" Thorn was grinning again. The red light of the interview recorder blinked merrily along with his clowning.

"We have evidence that suggests you may not be responsible for the murder of Kevin Wu," Hewson began.

"Of course you do. Like I said, I didn't kill Kevin." His smile widened further still.

"So why have you called us back in Julian? What is it that you want to say?" Hewson sighed.

"I know who *did* kill Kevin. And you do too," he nodded at Carson, grinning, "Shall we play a game?"

"No," said Hewson.

"Sure, why not," said Carson.

"Good," Thorn laughed, "So I kill four people - who stands to benefit?"

"No one. No one wins when someone is murdered," said Hewson forcefully.

"Sorry detective Hewson, that's the wrong answer,' Thorn made a quiz-show incorrect answer buzzing noise, "I'm afraid I'm going to have to hurry you for an answer DI Carson."

"The only benefit is to someone who wants to see Real Rock Restaurants fail," Carson was thinking out loud,

"But if you tell me the killer was Ronald McDonald, I'm going to punch you in the nose."

Thorn laughed. Hard. Hewson imagined Chapman hyperventilating outside the two-way mirror as his senior detective threatened violence towards a suspect.

"No, there's no clowns involved. Not clowns of the circus variety, anyway. Ha ha ha!"

"The only people who stand to benefit from a disaster like this are short-sellers," said Carson.

"Correct!"

"What's a short-seller?" asked Hewson, suddenly feeling like she was on the outside, that her Guvnor and the suspect were speaking a different language.

"It's a somewhat sketchy, but perfectly legal, investment technique," Carson explained, "Let's imagine you have 100 shares in RRR and I ask to borrow them for a little while. I'll even pay you a small convenience fee. Once you have given the shares to me, I immediately sell them on the open stock market. I'm gambling that the buy price of RRR shares falls, so when I buy 100 shares to give back to you, they cost less than what I sold them for. You get your 100 shares back and I pocket the profit."

"Very good DI Carson," Thorn was clapping quietly, "And the best thing about shorting is that the outlay is minimal, making it easy to generate a very healthy return for virtually zero initial investment."

"As long as the share price falls," Carson cautioned.

"As long as the share price falls," Thorn nodded in agreement.

Hewson had had enough, "So that's your defence? You're going to blame a shadowy hedge fund for the death of Kevin Wu? Perhaps this cabal hired a hitman to kill him so share prices would crash?"

"No, nothing as sinister as that detective," Thorn was enjoying himself as he toyed with them, "Basic human greed is more than enough motive, don't you think?"

"But you are not that greedy person?"

"Oh no, I have enough material possessions already, thanks," Carson paused for a moment before continuing, "Remember when I said I had obsessive tendencies? Once my brain latches onto something, I become completely fixated. So I quickly went from concerns about the music being played in Real Rock Restaurants to digging into every aspect of the business. I read *everything* I could. And as a financier, the stock market performance of RRR was of great interest."

Carson could feel the pieces falling into place, "So after the first murder, RRR share prices tumble. It's obvious that Paolo is not a run-of-the-mill murder but the actions of a lunatic, so a well-connected investor could easily predict another killing and another price fall in the foreseeable future. Someone selling borrowed shares before the death of Kirsten could almost guarantee a good return when they purchased the replacement RRR shares after the news broke."

"Bingo!" Thorn appeared to be pleased with Carson' progress, "But what if I told you someone came up with an even grander scheme once they realised what was going on?"

"Like?" Carson prompted him.

"Like someone who saw an opportunity to make a fortune *and* take a majority controlling stake in Real Rock Restaurants."

The penny dropped. "Oh," said Carson.

Misadvertised

Chapter Eighty-Nine

Although Real Rock Restaurants conducted their core hospitality business from a portfolio of stylish properties in highly desirable locations, the head office itself was spectacularly unimpressive. A stubby, red brick and dark glass office building crouching in the shadows of the Hammersmith flyover.

Carson again dumped his car directly outside the front door and marched into reception. Hewson followed, surprised by the clash between rock star memorabilia displays and the 1980s 'space age' architecture, all sharp glass triangles, red and black paint and a pathetic water feature in front of the reception desk. Carson was already in the receptionist's face, loudly demanding an immediate audience with Max Jackson.

The receptionist tried to calm him down, "I'm afraid Mr Jackson is in a meeting, Mr…?"

"*Detective Inspector* Carson," the policeman snarled, "Where is the meeting?"

"In the boardroom."

"Brilliant," Carson replied, heading for the lifts. Hewson was again left trailing in his wake, offering a weak, apologetic smile to the receptionist. Carson marched into the lift and jabbed the button for five, the top floor of the building.

"Do you even know where the boardroom is?" Hewson asked.

"On the top floor, obviously," he snapped leaning against the wall, panting, "An arrogant prick like Jackson wants to be master of all he surveys - and the top of the building is as good as it gets."

Hewson nodded. It made sense.

They arrived on the fifth floor and Carson strode off again, heading towards a glass-walled conference room that ran along one side of the building. Inside, Hewson could see the room was filled with a combination of staid beancounters wearing sensible clothing in muted colours and hip, creative types, all piercings, tattoos and half-shaved heads. Jackson was addressing the gathering from the front of the room, standing in front of a garish Powerpoint presentation projected onto the wall. Carson threw open the door at the end of the room and stood for a moment listening.

"The deaths of our colleagues are truly awful but rather than pretend nothing happened, we should promote their memory, allowing them to live on forever as part of the Real Rock Restaurant legend. Being known as the 'murder restaurant' will either make or break our brand, so I believe we should accept and embrace that reality. I propose pivoting towards a new image for Real Rock Restaurants that combines a growing consumer interest in dark tourism with our established rock-n-roll heritage. To that end, we have produced a new range of merchandise to commemorate each murder and the location…"

Misadvertised

"I've heard enough," Carson growled to Hewson before raising his voice so everyone in the conference room could hear, "You, Max Jackson, you're under arrest."

For the first time, Jackson noticed the two detectives at the rear of the room, "Oh hello detectives, ha ha, that's a good joke. But as you can see, I'm currently in the middle of a meeting. Perhaps you could arrange a meeting with my secretary?"

A young woman in a light coloured suit stood and began walking towards them, smiling shyly.

"Sorry Miss, we're in a bit of a hurry, trying to catch a killer," Carson shook his head at the secretary, "Max Jackson, I'm arresting you on suspicion of the murder of Kevin Wu. And some other stuff too."

Carson strode to the front of the room, span Jackson around and slapped a pair of handcuffs around his wrists.

"There's been a terrible misunderstanding," Jackson cried out to his board, "I'll have my secretary call you all to rearrange the rest of this meeting once I have sorted out this misunderstanding."

"No," Carson called back he steered Jackson through the office doorway, "He won't."

Chapter Ninety

Back in the car, Carson felt elated. They were inches away from closing the case. He called Eva to share the good news.

"It's me love," he said when she answered, "We've got a second suspect in custody. I think we're nearly done."

"That's great," Eva sounded distant and disinterested, "Really great James."

"So maybe I could take a few days off when I've finished the paperwork, spend some time together?"

"Yeah maybe."

Eva sounded spaced out. Carson wondered if the doctor had changed her medication again.

"OK, we can talk when I get home. I just wanted to give you the good news."

"Yeah, great, thanks. Bye."

Click. Bzzzzzzz.

"I love you, bye bye."

"I can tell you right now, she ain't going anywhere with you," Jackson crowed from the back seat, "She isn't even going to talk to you tonight."

Hewson spun round in her seat to face him, "Why don't you just shut up?"

Misadvertised

Chapter Ninety-One

By the time he had been transported back to Balls Pond Road, processed and cautioned, Jackson's entire demeanour had changed. The brash showman with the dodgy American accent had been replaced by a more cautious, guarded character whose eyes roamed the interview room, looking for some potential avenue of escape.

"Come on Carson," he wheedled, "you know it wasn't me. You confirmed my alibi with Dr Jenkins. I couldn't have killed Paolo."

"As I said when we arrested you Mr Jackson, we're here to talk about the killing of Kevin Wu."

"It wasn't me and you know it," he shook his head, "You've already arrested someone for the murders, so why are you harassing me?"

"Because aside from giving you the inspiration, we don't believe the other suspect had anything to do with the death of Kevin Wu. In fact, we have evidence that proves they did not," Carson was steady and measured, "But we do have strong evidence that *you* may be implicated. So I put it to you again, where were you on Sunday night?"

"At home. Alone."

"So no witnesses to corroborate your alibi?"

Misadvertised

"No. That's what alone means, detective," Jackson couldn't keep the sarcasm from his voice.

"Fine, we'll come back to that," Carson said. He looked at Hewson who passed him a sheaf of papers, "Tell me about Rocksteady Rhythm and Revenue."

"Who?"

"Don't pretend you've forgotten already Max," Hewson smiled sarcastically, "It's the firm you set-up last Wednesday afternoon. Remember? The one based in the Cayman Islands?"

She handed him a print out from the Cayman Islands Government, "From that sheet, could you please tell us the incorporation date and who the company directors are?"

Jackson glanced at the paper she handed him, "Wednesday 22nd. One director listed, Max Jackson."

"So that would be you Max. *You* set up a new offshore company called Rocksteady Rhythm and Revenue."

"Yes," he mumbled, "So?"

Hewson ignored him, instead passing over another sheet of paper, "This is a printout of stock market activity in Real Rock Restaurant shares on Wednesday 22nd and Thursday 23rd. You'll see that Rocksteady Rhythm and Revenue sold a large chunk of shares just before the market closed on Wednesday. Then, after news of the murder of Kirsten Grabowski circulated, Rocksteady Rhythm and Revenue bought back an even larger chunk of available shares. At a lower price, obviously."

"I believe it's called shorting," said Jackson sarcastically, "but I leave all that to my broker."

"*Money for Nothing* eh?" Carson matched his sarcasm, "The problem we have is that exactly the same thing happened after Ivan and Stacey were murdered in Soho on Friday." Jackson was handed another bundle of paper. He passed it to his solicitor unchecked.

"Like I said, this just appears to be my broker making some very shrewd decisions," he shrugged.

"Perhaps. But by Saturday afternoon, Rocksteady Rhythm and Revenue owned 47.2% of total Real Rock Restaurant stock. There was a *lot* of after market activity, but not quite enough for your investment firm to assume control."

"Is this going somewhere detective?" Jackson's solicitor asked.

"Yes," said Hewson, "Jail".

Carson ignored them both, "But the problem got worse, didn't it? You realised the killer wasn't coming back, that he was done. You needed one more big short to free up enough cash to buy enough shares to give you voting control - and the 'Ripper' wasn't going to do it for you."

Hewson picked up the thread, "You were so close to taking over - just not close enough. Without some psycho to do your dirty work, you were forced to do it yourself."

"And so you smashed Kevin Wu's head in a piano over and over and over again until he was a bloody pulp. Then you walked out and placed a buy order on Real Rock Restaurants ready for the stock market opening on Monday."

"That's a very interesting story detectives," said Jackson's brief, "But do you have any actual evidence to back it up? All these share transactions prove is that my client has an aggressive but smart stockbroker."

Jackson smirked.

"You mean apart from the biometric match of your client against the CCTV footage of the murder?" Asked Hewson, "How about the tiny drops of Kevin's blood that our SOCOs found in his car?"

"I gave Kevin a lift to work a while back. He had a nosebleed on the way," Jackson shrugged.

"Perhaps," Carson nodded, "What about the Kevin Wu murder display you have started assembling? It's very accurate - like it's ready for immediate installation in your Waterloo restaurant."

"We have to move fast in our industry. So when I heard about the latest murder, I checked the CCTV footage - remotely - then had my in-house design team spring into action. The same as they did for the murders of Paolo, Kirsten, Ivan and Stacy too."

"Well Mr Jackson, you seem to have an explanation for everything," Carson sighed, "Just one more question. How do you account for the small flecks of Kevin's brain tissue we found smeared into the stitching of your car's steering wheel."

Jackson stopped smiling and his fake orange tan turned an ashen grey.

"So why don't you just tell us what happened," Carson sighed.

"I need a few minutes with my client," the solicitor intervened.

Chapter Ninety-Two

In the end it was nearly half an hour before Jackson's solicitor came out to tell the detectives her client was ready to talk. Back in the interview room, all the colour had now drained from Jackson's face. He was a broken man.

Once Carson and Hewson were seated, Jackson lifted his weary head and fixed his gaze on them, "I killed Kevin Wu."

There was a muffled cheer from the corridor outside.

"I would also like to confess that I impeded your investigation."

"Really? I am surprised."

"From the moment I got the call about Paolo, I knew who the killer was."

"How?"

"I know him. I spoke to him. I encouraged him."

Hewson hadn't expected that.

"Who is 'him'?" Carson asked cautiously.

"Julian Thorn."

Hewson tried not to show her surprise.

"And how do you know Julian Thorn?"

"We worked tables together at the original Real Rock Restaurant many years ago, back when we were both at university. Thorn completed his degree and moved on, I dropped out of uni and worked my way up within the

Misadvertised

company. We lost touch after that, but he was always a bit of an odd, obsessive guy.

"Anyway, a few weeks ago, I bumped into him in the waiting room at Dr Jenkins' office. We got talking and it was clear that Julian had got worse. Told me he was seeing a therapist to try and manage his obsessive fixations. Apparently these fixations don't last long, but they are intense - each one taking over his life.

"We got to chatting about the olden days, working the tables at Real Rock Restaurants and our shared enjoyment of rock music. When I mentioned the fact that the restaurant playlist is now heavily skewed towards 21st Century pop music, it was like a switch flipped, told me that was downright wrong. That someone had to do something. He was getting more worked up by the minute.

"I suggested he visit his nearest RRR and see - hear - for himself. I could see he had money, was well connected, may be able to launch a social media campaign to take RRR back to its rock music roots or something. Maybe he'd write some letters to head office that I could use to sway the board. I admit, I goaded and inflamed him. But it never crossed my mind that his obsessive-compulsive problems may involve violence.

"I called him on the way to the restaurant the morning after Paolo was killed and told him he had to stop. He said he would - as soon as RRR started playing rock music again.

"When I arrived in Greenwich, there were dozens of onlookers trying to get a glimpse of the murder scene. They weren't sickened or disgusted or frightened - they were all seeking some grim kind of *thrill*. I was struck by the maddest idea - why not incorporate Paolo's murder into the Real Rock Restaurant legend? So I pretended I didn't know the meaning of Julian's message and I left the annoying pop tunes on the official playlist.

"The media circus got crazier with every killing, as did bookings at each of the murder scenes. The public were fascinated while the stock market reacted in horror. The investors missed it completely - profits were shooting up faster than the share price was falling. So with every killing, I got closer to my dream - total control of the Real Rock Restaurants brand.

"After Soho I still couldn't afford to buy the final tranche of shares. I needed just one more death - to acquire a controlling stake in the company and to cement the new RRR legend. But then DI Carson warned the RRR board about Julian's 'mission' - and they forced me to restore the original rock-only soundtrack.

"Julian must have been hanging around the restaurants and realised he'd achieved his goal because he sent me a text - 'Mission complete'. With rock music restored as the default RRR soundtrack, he could move onto his next crazy obsession. But that also meant he wouldn't be committing any more murders at my restaurants. He was done. So I was left holding a lot of shares for a business that would inevitably fail if I could not force through the strategic redirection.

"So I had to kill Kevin myself," Jackson began to sniffle.

"Bloody hell," Hewson muttered.

"Did you trade notes with Julian? Find out how to commit a true RRR murder?" Asked Carson.

"Hell no, he wouldn't have helped me. He had a mission and weirdly, anything beyond that would be morally objectionable to Julian. So I just watched the restaurant CCTV footage from Greenwich, Soho and Camden."

"Like a Youtube 'how to' video tutorial," Carson was appalled, "And you didn't seem to have much difficulty coming up with something equally graphic and horrific."

"I was shocked by how easy that part was once I decided what I was going to do. I guess when Dr Jenkins says there's a killer inside all of us, he's right."

"I sincerely hope you are wrong," said Carson, "What about Barry Green? Why did he have to do with anything? Why kill him?"

He was interrupted by a loud, persistent knocking on the door. A moment later a tall, blonde man in an expensive blue suit burst through the door.

"You," the interloper pointed at Jackson, "Not another word."

"You," he pointed at the solicitor, "Out. You're fired."

He turned his attention - and finger - to Carson, "And you, not another question until I have spoken with my client."

"Who are you exactly?" Jackson was as surprised as everyone else in the room.

"Not another word, I said," the man shook his finger at Jackson once more.

"Sir Anthony de Barge, I might have know it," Carson shook his head and stood up from the desk, "Come on Hewson, looks like we're done for now."

The two detectives followed the now-fired solicitor from the room, leaving de Barge alone with his client.

"You know that guy?" Hewson asked once they were safely out of earshot.

"I certainly do," Carson nodded, "and if you hang around criminal scum for long enough, you will too. They call him the Knight of Not Guilty. A truly slippery bastard who has helped far too many villains escape justice."

"Was it just me, or did Jackson looked surprised to see him?" Hewson asked.

"I expect de Barge has employed himself. He can't resist a high profile trial - and it doesn't get much bigger than a serial killer."

"So why isn't he representing the *actual* serial killer?"

"Now Hewson, *that* is a good question."

Misadvertised

Chapter Ninety-Three

"Yesterday I asked, 'Could the Met top the level of excitement?' And the answer is most definitely *yes!*"

Homes was manic, bouncing on his chair like a four year old child high on artificial food colourings and flavourings.

"First, the Balls Pond murder squad *finally* caught the Real Rock Restaurant Ripper, an individual named Julian Thorn, a quantitative analyst," Homes cupped a hand around his mouth and adopted a stage whisper, "*That's some kind of financial egghead.*"

Homes laughed loudly at his own joke before continuing, "Apparently Mr Thorn bore a slightly unusual grudge - he doesn't like pop music. Or more specifically, he doesn't like Real Rock Restaurants claiming to be a real rock restaurant chain - and then playing cheesy pop tunes. Now I'm not saying he's mental, but…"

Homes made a circular motion with a finger pointed at his head.

"As a special bonus, Thorn has made a full confession, bringing a swift conclusion to the case. Or does it…? What about my prime suspect, Max Jackson? Here's where it all gets a bit weird…"

Homes paused for dramatic effect, but his childlike bouncing up and down punctured the tension.

Misadvertised

"Thorn's confession only covered the first four murders - Paolo Nunez, Kirsten Grabowski, Ivan Yushenko and Stacey Kyle. He absolutely refused to accept responsibility for Kevin Wu."

Bounce, bounce, bounce. Homes was going to explode.

"But using his giant, twisted intellect, Thorn was able to point the police in the right direction - Max Jackson. It transpires that Kevin Wu was a copycat killing, carried out by Max as part of an audacious takeover attempt at Real Rock Restaurants. Wild huh?!"

"So in this case we got two killers for the price of one. Bet you didn't see that one coming - I certainly didn't."

"Unfortunately, any of you who had a flutter on Max Jackson in the Real Rock Ripper Gaming Room lose out this time. But anyone who selected 'Person Unknown', congratulations - we're paying out 2 to 1! A quick look at the stats suggests there aren't many of you though. Sorry."

"So that's it from me tonight. I'll be sure to share more updates as the case progresses, but don't forget, *everyone* is innocent until proven guilty in a court of law, including Max Jackson. And until his trial begins, Real Rock Restaurants have ended their sponsorship of the Homes on Homicide show. So if you're interested in becoming a patron, please drop me a line. Goodnight!"

Misadvertised

Chapter Ninety-Four

Ever since the dream, Woody had started to notice starlings everywhere. There were huge flocks of the little bastards all over London, swooping between trees and crapping on everything in sight. But it was the large group that congregated in the park near his shared flat that worried him most. He could hear them skittering across his roof in the mornings, squawking and scratching and pecking, trying to break through the felting. Perhaps that nutter on the incident room hotline had been right. Maybe they really were going to kill him.

He had been pissed to learn that starlings are protected under the Wildlife and Countryside Act 1981, meaning that the birds cannot simply be relocated. But what really annoyed Woody was that a junior environmental health officer over at Camden Borough Council had been the one to educate him on this particular law.

"So they're pests?" He had asked.

"Yes," the officer agreed.

"But you can't get rid of them?"

"Not really, no."

"So what are we supposed to do?"

"Do? You can't do anything sir, they are protected."

"But they are destroying the city. They carry diseases. They crap on everything…"

"There's no need for that kind of language sir. The starlings are protected, please leave them alone," the council mandarin cut the call.

Bloody stupid law, Woody thought to himself. He didn't want the birds killed, he just wanted them taken somewhere outside the city before *they* ended up killing someone. He'd googled every angle he could think of but the answer was always the same - you can't do anything, even if the birds are literally destroying your home.

He was about to give up for the evening when a notification popped up on his iPad screen:

```
Are you sick of unjust laws?
    Click to learn more.
             #
```

Woody knew Google's ad matching talents were scarily accurate, but this was the first time he'd ever seen anything like this. Intrigued, he tapped on the message, launching a very basic, text-only webpage.

```
             #
Welcome to the Citizen Action Network. We
are a group of normal, every day citizens.
   Normal, every day citizens who are sick of
unjust laws, unfair judgements and out-of-touch
                lawmakers.
  Normal, every day citizens who are ready to
              take action.
                Join us.
                   #
```

Woody clicked the button.

Misadvertised

Chapter Ninety-Five

Evan's phone pinged.

```
#
When we met last week, I didn't have a
chance to tell you - I love your accent :)
#
```

She stared at the message for a moment confused. Then she flushed. Was it Nicky Ninebar?

"Everything ok?" Hewson asked.

Evans reddened further, "Just an admirer. I think."

"Really? Anyone I know?"

"No," Evans was glad she didn't have to lie.

"Is it serious?"

Yes, but not in the way you mean, Evans thought to herself, "No, I barely know the guy."

"Well that could change. Text him back," Hewson nudged her.

"Yeah, maybe. I'll think about it," Evans tossed her phone into her bag.

Hewson arched her eyebrow quizzically, "OK, whatever."

"Anyway," Evans was desperate to change the subject, "What is going on with Carson? Is he using or what?"

"I don't think so," Hewson shook her head, "I know all is not well at home, but I don't he's the sort to mess with drugs. Or booze."

"What is 'not well at home'?" Evans probed.

"Come on Lisa, I'm his partner and I'm supposed to keep his confidences - just like you're supposed to keep Charlie's."

"Carson shares personal stuff with you?"

"No of course not," Hewson shook her head again, "I'm not sure Carson is capable of emotional vulnerability - with me or anyone else. All I know is things are very rocky with his wife. Oh, and he *really* hates jazz music."

"I can understand that," Evans shrugged, "OK fine, so you don't want to talk about Carson. How are *you* doing?"

"I've been worse," Hewson looked down at the table, "But I still hate going home. Everything is always so quiet now…"

Evans said nothing, just clasped Hewson's hand and sat in silence while her colleague suffered a wave of grief and regret. Eventually she spoke again, "Have you heard anything from traffic? Did they ever make any progress?"

"No, nothing," Hewson wiped her eyes, "It's just a hit and run for them. No quick win, so they're not interested in devoting more resources to tracking the car. Besides, they are far too busy chasing the guys who keep cutting down the ULEZ cameras."

Evans nodded. Masked protestors calling themselves 'bladerunners' had been destroying the cameras used to police - and tax - cars coming into London. City Hall had expected the trend to end quite quickly, but the blade runners were still busy, destroying several cameras every week. The problem was, Met Police resources kept getting diverted into investigating the vandalism - dragging them away from cases like David's.

"Are you still running your own investigation?" She asked.

Hewson nodded and sighed, "As much as I can, not that I've had a decent lead in weeks. I just read the case file over and over and over, but there's never anything new. So now I'm just hoping – praying – to stumble across a silver ID.4."

"Maybe one of these days we'll get lucky."

"Not if you don't text that guy back you won't," Hewson said with a wink.

Chapter Ninety-Six

Witz was walking back from the corner shop to his bedsit when a large Mercedes drew alongside. The rear passenger window rolled down an impressively moustachioed face leaned out.

"Ah Detective Witz, do you have a moment," Sahin smiled.

"Not really, no," Witz shook his head, desperate to get inside and open the bottle of whisky he'd just bought.. Something was very wrong.

"That wasn't actually a request," Sahin's smile grew wider, "Hop in, we're going for a drive."

The street was deserted, there was no one to call out to. No one to see him getting into a London gangster's car. He wasn't sure if that was a good thing or not. Shrugging to himself, he climbed into the back of the Mercedes and tried to settle himself as the car pulled away from the kerb. Sahin stared out the window for a few minutes, watching the London lights streak by. Finally he spoke, "I hear congratulations are in order. Your team solved the case and caught the killer. I want to thank you for removing this animal from the streets."

Witz nodded, waiting to find out what was going on. Sahin said something in Turkish and the man in the front passenger seat turned to face Witz. He stared at the detective for a moment, nodded and said "*Evet.*"

"So Detective Witz, it seems we have two things to celebrate today," Sahin spoke again, "You captured a man who was disrupting my business in Greenwich *and* you have landed yourself a new job."

Witz shook his head, "Sorry Sahin, I think you've been misinformed, no new job for me."

"Oh, but that is where *you* are misinformed, Detective," Sahin's teeth glittered in the half light, "You *do* have a new job. Working for me."

The Turk chuckled. It was probably the second worst sound Witz had ever heard after Barry's neck breaking.

"I'm not for sale Sahin," Witz said.

"Again, this is not a request," Sahin was suddenly deadly serious, "Unless you want to go to prison for killing Barry Green?"

Witz choked. He felt as though someone had just punched him the gut.

"Yes, Detective Witz, I know about Barry Green. I know that you killed him. I know that you threw his body into the sewers."

"You know nothing," Witz tried to hide his shock with bluster.

"And I know that you never reported the incident. *I know your secret Charlie.*"

Witz stared at Sahin. He felt a deep rage and an even deeper fear.

"The man in the front seat? He also works for me, doing some of the more unpleasant tasks that need to be done. At the moment he is on holiday 'lying low' because there is a little too much police scrutiny of his most recent job."

Sahin paused, the playful smile back. "And do you know *where* my man has been holidaying?"

Witz stared at the gangster in stony silence.

"He's been camping Detective Witz. In the Catacombs. I believe you found his accommodation when you were poking around down there the other day."

This was it, Witz was screwed.

"This man saw what happened Charlie. And unlike anyone else, he believes it was an accident, that you never meant to kill Barry. You're a good officer with a decent reputation and a long history of outstanding service; why would you want to murder a man you didn't even know?"

"No, you're not a murderer Charlie," Sahin smiled wickedly, suddenly very friendly "I agree with my man, I think the man's death was just a terrible mistake. And I will be happy to keep your secret just between the two of us now you are working for me."

"But there are three of us…" Witz began to protest. He fell silent as, in one smooth move, Sahin leant forward and slit the throat of the man in the passenger seat. Blood sprayed everywhere, covering the car and its occupants. Witz could feel droplets on his face and neck.

"Two of us," Sahin snarled handing the knife to Witz, "Now I have had to sacrifice one of my best men to make sure you understand what I am saying. You do understand, don't you Charlie?"

Witz nodded dumbly. Sahin took the knife back from Witz and dropped it into a plastic ziplock bag which disappeared into his tracksuit jacket pocket. The Mercedes pulled to halt outside Witz's flat, they must have been driving in circles.

"Now get out," Sahin nodded towards the door, "I'll be in touch."

Witz stood silently on the pavement, watching the Mercedes accelerate away into the night.

He was screwed.

Chapter Ninety-Seven

"Solving five murders and catching two killers on your return to active duty - that's a pretty impressive first few weeks back in the job," Chapman said, giving Carson a congratulatory slap on the back, "Remember the good old days when we would've been allowed to have a few fingers of scotch to celebrate the end of a case like this?"

"Feels like a lifetime ago, Guv," Carson mumbled, "As for Jackson, I'm not convinced we would have got him without Thorn pointing us in the right direction."

"But you got the right result and Jackson will be held on remand until he's brought to trial. Seriously Carson, well done. Even that useless bastard the Mayor is impressed."

Carson nodded wearily, "We're no closer with finding out who killed Barry Green though. Neither Jackson nor Thorn are admitting to it."

"Do you think one of them is lying?"

"Either of them *could* have done it, but my gut says no."

"Maybe it was just a weird coincidence and Barry *did* die accidentally. Very occasionally they do happen. And Barry's body was so smashed up after passing through the London sewers that the pathologist couldn't confirm whether his death was an accident or not anyway,"

Chapman shrugged, "Regardless, you should go home Carson. Get some rest, see the departmental shrink, spend some time with the wife."

Carson winced.

"Things still not improving? Do you want me to talk to her, explain where you've been and what your sacrifice, *her* sacrifice, was for?"

Carson shook his head, hoping his boss couldn't see the tears that were welling up in his eyes.

"I'm sorry James," this time Chapman placed a gentle hand on his subordinate's shoulder, "And I'm sorry for what living undercover has done to your wife."

"Let's just say that everything I lived through in those two years was *nothing* in comparison to what I'm going through now," Carson croaked, "Violence, drugs, perversion, squalor, filth, hate, indifference, none of it a patch on slowly losing your wife as she processes the lies."

Chapman gave his shoulder another gentle squeeze.

"Look, I hate to add to your misery right now, but professional standards are looking into the Charlie Kingston shooting. MO19 say you were jumpy, erratic and out of control and the initial report claims your intervention was a significant influencing factor in the officer's decision to open fire. They've closed ranks and are blaming you."

"Bollocks," Carson started angrily, "I tried to stop the shooting. Check their bloody body cams if you don't believe me."

"I know, I did and I do James, but my hands are tied," Chapman nodded sadly, "You've been 'out of sight' for two years and, despite your stellar work undercover, the brass have forgotten you - so they're siding with Sergeant Turner and his brown nose. Now the word has come down from on high - I have to move you away from the front line for a while."

"To where?"

"N1C."

"N1C is real? I thought it was just a story chief constables told their new recruits to keep them in line."

"No, it exists alright and you start Monday. I'll text you the address. Turn up, do your time, keep your head down and I'll bring you back here as soon as I can. Hewson will keep your seat warm in the meantime. I'm sorry James, but that's the way it has to be for now."

Carson stood and gave his boss a desultory nod as he shuffled unsteadily from the office.

"And whatever you're doing, stop it. Senior brass has ordered unannounced drugs testing next week," Chapman called out as his detective wandered down the corridor leading to the carpark, "Speak to your shrink or something. Get yourself sorted."

Carson waved dismissively over his shoulder and kept walking.

Before you go…

I sincerely hope you enjoyed reading *Misadvertised* as much as I did writing it.

If you did, could I please ask a favour - leave me a quick review to say what you did (or did not) like about the story? Your reviews make all the difference to us indie authors - without them, no one finds (or reads) our books. And for some of us, that means we can't afford to eat…

These links will take you direct to the relevant review page:
US: https://www.amazon.com/review/create-review?&asin=B0CR5STG46
UK: https://www.amazon.co.uk/review/create-review?&asin=B0CR5STG46
Australia: https://www.amazon.com.au/review/create-review?&asin=B0CR5STG46
GoodReads: https://www.goodreads.com/book/show/204476273-the-warsaw-gambit

If you really, really enjoyed the story, how about letting a friend know? You could even buy them a copy if you're feeling super generous:

1. Go to the *Misadvertised* eBook's product detail page on Amazon.

2. In the **Buy for others** box select the quantity you want to purchase.
3. Select the **Buy for others** button and then enter the details for your gift recipients. If you didn't provide a recipient email address, instructions on how to manage your books are emailed to you after the order is complete.

Thanks again for for taking the time to read *Misadvertised*.

Benjamin Lloyd

DI Carson will return in *Misrepresented*.

About the author

As a child at primary school, Benjamin Lloyd was regularly sent on creative writing classes by his teachers. So naturally he went on to study forensic science before falling into a career in IT.

Some years later, he returned to what he does best - words. Working as a freelance copywriter for global IT brands he has written millions of words to help sell computers, software and services. In between ebooks and advertorials, he also writes a successful travel blog, *Journey into Darkness*, with his wife Linda.

Misadvertised is Benjamin's second novel.
He lives in Essex, UK with his enormous family.

Find out more at:
https://www.tech-write.co.uk
https://www.journeyintodarkness.co.uk

Other books by Benjamin Lloyd:

The Warsaw Gambit

Russia has invaded Ukraine. Europe is in chaos. And NATO refuses to get involved.

Faced by overwhelming military might and dwindling support from its allies, Ukraine is about to fall. And the rest of Eastern Europe could be next.

Then a long-dead Cold War era double agent makes contact with his CIA handler, sharing a secret that could end the war. So why does no one want to act?

Taking the initiative, the Polish government arranges a simple mission with a team of five volunteers. All they have to do is find - and kidnap - the Russian president.

But time is running out...

In the tradition of Gerald Seymour and Frederick Forsyth, *The Warsaw Gambit* will keep you gripped until the final page.

Can a five-man team of volunteers succeed in stopping Russia or is Europe condemned to repeat the mistakes of the past?

Misadvertised

The Warsaw Gambit is available now. Turn the page to read a sample…

The Warsaw Gambit

Chapter 1

Jankowski was shaking. He felt like he had just seen a ghost. He looked at his hastily scribbled notes and realised he may not have seen one, but he had definitely *heard* from one.

And now it was his turn to come back from the dead.

Despite the automatic glance to his left, Warner almost missed the signal, two yellow chalk stripes on the side of Church of the Holiest Saviour on Zbawiciela Place. Hardly surprising though, the Cold War had ended nearly thirty-five years ago, all of his contacts long since retired. Enjoying the luxuries of imperialist capitalism no doubt. Unless they had died of course. He only came this way from a 30-something year old habit, a slight detour on his way to buy a newspaper and milk from the Żabka grocery store down the block from his apartment. The same steps, the same sideways glance, the same sense of disappointment when there was nothing to see. And yet today…

He took another look, convinced the stripes must be some kind of coincidence, just local kids messing around. But there they were, fresh, two bold yellow lines clearly visible on the crumbling grey concrete. It had to be a joke because the man behind the chalk was dead, had been for decades.

Having nothing better to do, he brushed the chalk off with his sleeve and walked on towards Park Belwederski and the long-dead dead drop his long-dead contact had used to pass SB secrets. *For old times sake*, he muttered grinning to himself as he walked through the wrought iron gates. At least it would give someone a laugh, even if it was at his expense. Maybe he was about to be the star of a new CIA hidden camera show.

It was already mid-morning but the sun was weak and a light mist hovered above the carefully manicured lawns. Joggers and dog walkers weaved their way through the trees, appearing and disappearing in the damp fog and shadows, casting long shadows across the dew fringed leaves.

Warner made his own meandering trek through the park, darting behind hedges and doubling back to check if he was being followed. *Old habits*, he smiled, approaching a low retaining wall behind an empty flowerbed. He was wheezing with exertion, and his forehead was damp with sweat under the battered brown homburg he wore. His waistline expansion was inversely proportional to his level of fitness, so Warner took the opportunity to catch his breath and carry out a final check for watchers. Satisfied he wasn't being observed, he pulled a damp, mossy brick from the wall and felt in the space behind. He didn't honestly expect to find anything, but who doesn't like to collect assorted filth under their fingernails?

He jumped as his fingers brushed against something in the hole then, pulse quickening, forced himself to grab hold of the mystery object. But it wasn't a mystery, it was a small metal tube. He unscrewed it to extract a small, rolled-up piece of very thin tissue paper - but he already knew what it said.

A broad smile spread across his chubby face. *Just like the good old days*. But how?

His brain was still sharp, but he was completely out of practice so it had taken him some time to remember the correct rules of a meet. Originally he had planned to arrive fifteen minutes early to check the location for surveillance but then he remembered that there wouldn't be any. It was hardly likely that Jankowski would be under observation - the man was long dead. The SB had been disbanded in 1989 when democracy had finally arrived in Poland, so there were no secret police to worry about either. No one would care about an old Cold War warrior like him either - assuming they even recognised him. This had to be an elaborate joke by another bored old man like himself. Maybe one of the old crowd from Warsaw Station playing a trick.

At 4pm he opened the door to the bar and immediately spotted Jankowski sat at a table in the shadows at the back of the room. Clichéed? Perhaps. But that's because it works.

The long room was quite full, students piling in from the nearby Politechnika Warszawska as lectures finished for the day. All of the tables and chairs were occupied and there was a crush of thirsty undergraduates waiting at the bar. The grey heads of Warner and Jankowski would have been quite conspicuous if the SB had still been on the look out for capitalist spies. But now they could pass for ageing academics out for an extracurricular drink.

Jankowski stood as Warner approached his table. He was the epitome of average - average height, average grey hair, average looks, average clothes. Indeed, his complete lack of remarkableness is exactly why he had been so successful in his work for the SB - and his CIA handlers. The only thing that wasn't average was his sharp, unblinking eyes that missed nothing. He had barely changed at all since they had last met.

"The waiter recommends the pierogi," Jankowski opened, his face betraying no emotion at all.

"Today I have a taste for gołąbki," countered Warner.

They stared at each other for a moment, then burst into laughter. Jankowski grabbed Warner and embraced him, slapping him on the back, before nudging his towards the bench on the opposite side of the table. "Your accent is still terrible. But I have missed you my old friend. How have you been? I thought you had returned to America?"

"I did, for a few years. But it seems I went native, your miserable city is in my blood. I've been living here for a quarter of a century now."

"And you never thought to visit me for vodka?" Jankowski asked, pretending to be offended.

"Probably because you are dead. I read the reports myself."

"Even though most Poles just wanted to forget everything that happened, some wanted 'justice'. So they started hunting down former SB agents. 'Dying' seemed like a good way not to *die*."

"Thank God."

"Thank God indeed."

"So, what brings me here today? You just wanted to see if the CIA was still active in Warsaw? Maybe find someone to talk with about the old days?"

"*Nie*, I have important news. *Really* important intel," Jankowski was completely deadpan.

I doubt it, Warner thought, stroking his chin in the universal sign of disbelief. "You can't have known that I would see the dead drop signal? Or that I would act - you're dead after all."

"*Nie*, I just hoped that someone from Warsaw Station would recognise the old ways. I needed to get someone's attention - and I did not know you were still here."

Misadvertised

"Important intel? Why not stop by the embassy? You know you're allowed to just walk in there these days, right?"

"I tried. I went to Ujazdowskie and asked to speak to a field agent, but they refused. No one would listen. No one cares. They didn't believe me."

"OK," sighed Warner, "So what is it? What didn't they believe?"

"I know how to end the war in Ukraine before it spreads or turns nuclear. Because I know *exactly* where Leontin will be on April 27th. Maybe they will listen to you."

Warner had nearly laughed in the old man's face. But the longer they talked, the clearer it became that Jankowski was telling the truth. His intel had always been good, completely accurate and even thirty something years later he was still on the ball.

According to Jankowski's source, Leontin had an important meeting scheduled at the President's official dacha at Dolgiye Borody, a small village about halfway between Moscow and Saint Petersburg. Built for Stalin, although it is said that he hated the silence of the countryside so much he only visited once. It took five years to build, using the same design as his dacha at Volyn but he…"

"We can talk about Stalin's hatred of spruce forests another time," Warner interrupted, steering Jankowski back on topic, "Tell me about this meeting."

"My source does not know why, but Leontin believes the meeting is so important and so sensitive that is must be held in person in a place he feels safe. The date cannot be changed so Leontin *has* to be there."

"Who is he meeting?" Warner pushed, "Who holds that much power over him?"

"I don't know because my source did not say. Maybe my source does not know yet. But it's big. Important. Top secret and essential. That is what my source is telling me, *essential*"

"And who is your source?"

"You still ask the same questions after all these years! But this time if I tell you it was the elderly housekeeper at the dacha you would not believe me."

"Is it the elderly housekeeper at Dolgiye Borody?"

"Yes, of course!"

Jankowski was right, Warner did not believe him. He had never figured out where the old SB man got his information. His sources were always anonymous and their contact infrequent - but they were never wrong. Warner had built his career on them, so they had to be highly placed - and trusted - in the Russian government.

Working with Langley, Warsaw Station had tried, and failed, to identify any of Jankowski's sources in the hope of establishing direct contact. But Jankowski had always been a smart player, each drop containing nothing more than the most important details to protect his sources - and to keep himself in the loop.

So despite his impeccable track record, it was now up to Warner to convince the CIA to take Jankowski's bombshell seriously. *Fat chance*, he thought, *they're just going to laugh their asses off.*

"As much as I enjoyed the dead drop, I guess it's redundant now," said Warner, "Why don't we just agree to meet back here at the same time tomorrow? Then I can tell you what the Agency have decided to do."

"*Nie*, we will meet at my apartment and drink vodka. I hope they kill the bastard."

They shook hands, grinning like kids. They were back in the game.

Back in his own apartment, Warner looked at the clock. It would be 11am in Langley so he could pass on the message without getting anyone out of bed. Even if it turned out to be the useless ramblings of an old man who missed the thrills of the past, at least he wasn't going to piss anyone off. He dialled through to the Europe desk in the ugly, squat building back Stateside.

The young analyst who took the call had no idea who Warner was. He could hear her tap-tapping his access codes into her computer followed by a sigh of exasperation when his name and credentials were verified. He could imagine the young woman rolling her eyes in frustration at a colleague on the desk opposite. Switching to an encrypted line, Warner was invited to share his intel. The analyst scribbled the details onto her notepad before promising to pass the info to Russia desk team for actioning. Her second promise of a return call was even less convincing.

Chapter 2

Warner was roused by a persistent knocking on his door. He had waited all night by the phone waiting for Langley to call back, eventually falling asleep in his threadbare armchair as the first shafts of dawn sunlight peeked around the edges of his faded and tatty curtains.

He rubbed the sleep from his bleary eyes and stumbled to the door of his apartment. He was surprised to find a well-dressed young American man waiting impatiently.

"Can I come in and have a word? I'm here from Warsaw Station," he said, sharp and business-like.

Warner gestured towards the small sitting room on the left, encouraging the young man to take a seat on the sofa, "Tea?"

The analyst looked in disgust at the aged furniture and shook his head. He had been told to stroke the old man's ego, to make him feel valued. Quite the star when he was an agent thanks to a source who seemed to have a direct line to the Kremlin. He had glanced at Warner's file and career track record before making the visit, but the truth was he didn't care for these old Cold War warriors and their insane conspiracy theories. He looked again at the cluttered bookshelves, dusty sills and dog-eared beige wallpaper. The old bastard had let himself go, maybe he'd actually gone native.

He shook his head again. "No, thank you. Listen, I won't take up too much of your time Mr Warner," he began, "I just wanted to let you know that the Agency is thankful for your efforts yesterday and we will take it from here. Although the Russia desk at Langley was more than a little annoyed at the way you breached protocol."

He was oily and unconvincing, greasy as his slicked-back hair and unable to keep the condescending tone out of his voice as he relayed their displeasure.

"Naturally." The young man's disinterest and disrespect irritated Warner and he knew he was about to be dismissed by this jumped-up little prick in his designer suit and handmade Italian leather shoes.

"Naturally. We don't really expect much from this one, the Cold War has been over for decades after all. But we'll pass it up the chain, so to speak." The man just wanted to leave, to get out of this filthy time warp he found himself in.

"Naturally," said Warner again. "And if Jankowski tries to make contact again?"

"We'll take a look at what he's given us first. If it's any good, then one my team will take over running the asset. Personally I doubt there will be anything to do."

"Naturally."

"Anyway, thanks again for your help," the young, nameless man said. "I'll see myself out."

He started walking towards the door and then

paused, "Oh, one other thing Mr Warner. Langley was very clear. I must warn you, whatever happens, you are to leave it to the the serving officers."

"Naturally."

And just like that, the annoying young man was gone.

Two men huddled around a desk in a small, poorly-lit office in the Kremlin.

"It seems that Jankowski has reactivated himself in Warsaw," the younger of the men said, passing a short printout to the blue-suited man on his left.

"Should we be worried?" Alexey Sokolov was the head of the Presidential Security Service, SPB for short. A small sub-directorate dedicated to a single task - protecting the Russian president. Which is probably why he looked like a bouncer, short brown hair, broad shoulders and a nose that looked like it had been battered a few times.

"He was a serious problem in the 80s and 90s. A devious bastard too, always had accurate intel sourced from the highest levels of the KGB and other government agencies," the younger man continued, "We'd never have identified him if the Americans hadn't been so lazy after Perestroika."

"Why did we not deal with him then?"

"Because apparently *we* were lazy bastards too. That and the fact he died before we got to him anyway"

Printed in Great Britain
by Amazon

45033481R00175